Blood Gravity

a novella

Gayle Towell

Blue Skirt Productions

Published 2014 by Blue Skirt Productions

blueskirtproductions.com/blue-skirt-press

The Blue Skirt logo is a trademark of Blue Skirt Productions

Copyright © 2014 by Gayle Towell

gayletowell.com/bloodgravity

All rights reserved.

No part of this book may be reproduced or transmitted in any form or by any electronic or mechanical means, including photocopying, recording, or by any information storage and retrieval system, without written permission of the author, except where permitted by law.

Names, characters, places, and incidents are the products of the author's imagination or are used fictitiously. Any resemblance to actual events, locales, or persons, living or dead, is entirely coincidental.

Book design by Gayle Towell

Interior artwork by Marylea M. Quintana Madiman

ISBN 978-0-9907654-0-0

First Edition

Printed in the United States of America

WARNING: This novella contains material and deals with subject matter that may be triggering to some. For more details and links to resources visit gayletowell.com/triggerwarnings.

Blood Gravity

CHAPTER ONE

My bedroom door creaks open in the middle of the night, waking me, making my heart beat up in my throat. For a second, I'm twelve again, and the only person who might push the door open at this hour would be Dad. But the shadow I see backlit by the hall light is too short. And I'm twenty, not twelve—home from college for the weekend.

Small footsteps cross the room, and soon there's a whisper. "Jake?"

It's Benny, my five-year-old brother. But the tightness in my chest doesn't ease. "What are you doing?" I say. "It's the middle of the night."

"Mom wouldn't let me stay up and say hi."

"I got in pretty late," I say.

He folds his arms on the mattress and rests his chin there, staring at me in the dark with sleep-messed brown hair.

"Go back to bed." I close my eyes and try to take a deep breath. "We'll hang out in the morning."

He moves closer and whispers, "I had a accident."

I sigh. "Again?"

"I didn't even drink any water. I don't know how it happened."

I sit up, leaving the warm comfort of my blankets for the cold house. Dad always turns the thermostat too low at night. I rub my face.

"Are you mad?" Ben whispers.

I want to say, *You need to stop pissing the bed like a damn toddler, already,* but I'm pretty sure that would make him cry. So instead, I say, "No, I'm not mad."

"Mom gets mad. Don't tell her, okay?"

"I won't. Let's get you cleaned up."

As I follow him out of my room in the dark, I stub my toe on one of the dozen boxes scattered around and have to bite my tongue not to curse in front of the kid. Ever since I left for college, Mom started storing all sorts of random crap in here. Old books, clothes, pictures, Christmas decorations. A broken microwave. I'm pretty sure the box I just hit my toe on is filled with tools Dad never uses.

I lead Ben across the hall into the bathroom and flick on the light. The entire front of his green dinosaur pajama bottoms are soaked as he stands on Mom's pristine linoleum, looking at me with big, sad eyes of shame, holding his hands together in front of his crotch like that might hide it. I grab a folded washcloth out of a drawer, wet it with warm water, add soap, and hand it to him.

"Strip and wipe," I say. "I'll get you some clean PJs."

Then I leave him, go to his room, and a sharp pain shoots

Blood Gravity

up the arch of my foot as I step on the head of a plastic dinosaur before turning the light on. This time I let "fuck" slip out between my teeth. The kid's room is a mess—dinosaurs, trucks, and Legos all over the floor. Mom always makes him clean his room before bed so this must all be from some late-night play session because he couldn't sleep.

But I don't care about the toys. It's become subconscious reflex to do a quick survey for beer bottles like the ones Dad used to leave in my room when I was a kid. There are none. There's never been. Nothing amiss here but bedding full of kid piss.

I strip his bed and load the washing machine in the hall closet. I find blue pajama pants and a Superman t-shirt in his dresser and bring them to the bathroom where I find him stripped naked and shivering.

"I'm so, so, so, so cold," he says.

"These'll warm you up." I set the dry clothes on the lid of the toilet, grab his wet clothes and the washcloth off the floor, and add them to the wash.

Ben comes back out into the hallway, dressed, arms wrapped around himself, still shivering. "Can I sleep with you?" he asks.

"You're getting kind of old for that, aren't you?" Then I mumble, "Also getting kind of old for wetting the bed."

"Please?" His eyes water, and his bottom lip quivers as he shivers.

I sigh. "Fine. As long as you promise not to pee on me."

"I promise," he says, rubbing his face with his sleeve.

We go back to my room. I lie on my back, and he lies on his side, his ice cold feet on my legs, grabs my arm with one hand, shoves his thumb in his mouth and closes his eyes. He's fast asleep in seconds, but that jolt of anxiety I felt when the door opened still buzzes in the background, and I spend the rest of the night staring at the ceiling in the dark, letting my eyes focus and unfocus. Shapes and shadows move around, and I try to control them. Eventually, it becomes light outside.

When I hear movement around the house, I get out of bed. I find Mom in the hallway opening the washing machine. Pink bathrobe tied at the waist. Dark hair unbrushed. She pulls out Ben's bedding and looks at me with a pursed-lip smile.

"I promised him I wouldn't tell," I whisper and fold my arms for warmth.

"I don't know why he still does this," she says.

"I think he was up late playing."

"You know he cried last weekend when you didn't come home."

"I couldn't. Too much homework."

"I know," she says. "That's what I told him. But he misses you." She looks back at the wet laundry as her shoulders drop. "He still has accidents during the day, too. And he hides it and tries to pretend it didn't happen. He's supposed to start kindergarten in the fall. He can't do that at school."

"He's still got five months. Maybe he'll grow out of it by then."

"He still sucks his thumb," she adds, looking me right in the eye.

She's doing that thing where she unloads her worries onto me in one fell swoop like maybe I can work towards rectifying it all while I'm here. Ever since Ben was born, my status in this house changed from child to third parent.

"He'll stop," I say. Because maybe magic will happen.

"It's your father," she says. "He babies him too much."

As if on cue, my parents' bedroom door opens. Dad emerges in boxer shorts and a t-shirt, grinning. He tries to lock eyes with me, but I look away. Every muscle in my body tenses as he saunters down the hall. He reaches out when he gets close, grabs my shoulder and hugs me.

His arms are warm, and I almost want to linger. Dad is a force like gravity. I roll downhill to him. And yet I want to be free of him. Or I know that's what I should want. But outside of his reach is a great, dark nothing.

By the time he releases me, the feeling has progressed to a sense of contamination and self-loathing. My chest is tight, and I want to run, but I just stand there as that feeling burrows. I stare at Mom fussing with the laundry.

"How late did you get in?" Dad says in the passive way he speaks when he already knows the answer.

Mom responds per her programming. "It was after ten."

"You sleep good?" he says.

"Yeah," I say, per my programming.

"And how's school?"

"Good." I nod.

"That's what I like to hear."

It's what he expects to hear. I've always been a good student, and he's always taken ownership in it. He's always been there to nudge, hint, approve and disapprove of all minor things in just the right way so as to make me into exactly what he intended. The obedient son. The perfect student. I suppose that's what parents do, but sometimes I wonder where his ideas end and mine begin.

"You pick a major yet?" he says.

Gayle Towell

"I've got until the end of the term before I need to decide," I say.

"Is it still between History and Math?"

Mom says, "Why don't you just double major?" She holds Ben's bedding, half of it snaked into the dryer, the other half in her hands.

"They're entirely different fields, Mom. Do you know what my course load would be like next year if I did that?"

Ben comes out of my bedroom just then, hugs Dad around the legs, hugs Mom around the legs, then stands by me and puts his thumb in his mouth. Mom looks at the thumb sucking, then to me. So I pat Ben's shoulder and say, "Thumb?" and he takes it out of his mouth.

"You're going to ruin your teeth, Pumpkin," Mom says, petting his head like he's a cat.

Dad says, "They're just baby teeth, Helen."

I would defend Mom by mentioning that the position of the baby teeth can, in fact, affect the position of adult teeth, but this discussion is about Dad asserting his dominance, not about getting the right answer.

Dad reaches out and lifts Ben up into his arms. "Ugh," he jokes. "You're getting too heavy for this."

Ben laughs as Dad carries him off into the kitchen. I nod at the laundry. "I'll get it, Mom."

She smiles, pats my arm, and says, "Thanks," before following Ben and Dad.

After I start the dryer I find Ben in the kitchen standing on a chair, mixing pancake batter as Dad heats a pan on the stove. I get a glass of water.

The fridge is covered in Ben's crayon and marker

Blood Gravity

drawings. Every time I come home, there are new ones. He's been drawing a lot of trees, lately. And dinosaurs and rivers with fish. Like always, and with little thought, I check to make sure nothing disturbing is showing up in his art. It all looks perfectly benign.

The thermostat is turned up and the house starts to warm. The whole place smells like Mom's favorite vanilla candles.

I flop on the peach floral sofa and Ben looks into the living room from his chair in the kitchen and says, "See? I can make pancakes now. I'm mixing it all up."

"Yeah, I see. You'll be ready to move out on your own soon," I say.

Ben holds a scoop, and Dad guides his hand, scooping up batter and carefully dropping it in the pan. Ben looks back at me again, smiling.

Mom sits at the table, reading the newspaper. "Remember all that smoke and fire trucks we saw yesterday?" She looks at Dad. He looks back, waiting. "A house burned to the ground. They didn't have working smoke detectors. A man died," she says.

"A man died?" Ben says.

"Helen," Dad says. "Why are you even reading that?"

"When was the last time we checked our smoke detectors?" she says.

Dad sighs, "Our smoke detectors are fine. You're worrying too much again." He disappears down the hall, and comes back with a pill in his palm, plops it down on the table in front of Mom, then brings her a glass of water. Valium. She swallows it down without question.

Soon the smell of warm pancakes overcomes the vanilla, and I help Mom set the table. Once we're all seated, Ben watches us closely as we take our first bites and nod in approval. He gets up on his knees in his seat so he can be as tall as the rest of us.

"We went to kindergarten ornamentation last week," he says.

"Ornamentation?" I say.

"Orientation," Mom corrects.

Ben says, "Yeah. I meeted my teacher and other kids. I showed her I can read some words."

"You *met* your teacher," Mom corrects again. "No baby talk."

Ben looks to Dad, and Dad offers Mom a glare of disapproval.

"What words can you read now?" I say.

"Um, dog, cat, go, stop, see, and, the, exit, mom, dad, brother, and I know how to sound some out, too. And I know fart," he grins. "F-A-R-T."

"Sounds like you're almost ready for college," I say.

"I'm going to go to your school when I get bigger," he says.

Mom watches my plate, likely performing a calculation of the percentage of my food I've eaten. Probably estimating the calories and extrapolating what the daily total would be if I ate at this rate for all meals. Her mouth opens, she draws in a breath, and I know her words before she says them.

"Are you eating enough at school? You seem very thin."

"He's fine," Dad says, patting my shoulder, making it so with his words.

After Mom looks down and forks a bite of pancake, Ben says, "I'm almost ready to not have training wheels on my bike no more."

"Is that so?" I say.

Blood Gravity

"Uh-huh. And did you know I can do plus?"

"Plus?" I say.

"Like three plus four is seven. Dad showed me."

Mom smiles to herself like she had a happy thought. Then she looks at me and says, "What was the name of that girl in your psychology class?"

"Rachel," I say.

"Is she nice?"

"I guess," I say.

Dad puts his elbows on the table, sits tall, and says, "Leave him alone, Helen. He's at school to learn."

Then Ben pipes up with, "Dad taked me to his work and showed me where he makes the medicines."

"He doesn't make the medicines, Benny," I say. "He dispenses them."

"What's dispenses?"

"He gives the medicines to the people who need it. People get notes from their doctors, and Dad gives them the right medicines."

"I know that already," he says. "That's a pharmacist."

"Eat your breakfast, Pumpkin," Mom says, and Ben takes another bite.

After we eat and clear the table, Ben runs into the living room, makes a *shuuuck* sound and curls into a ball on the floor. "Pretend you just saw a egg," he says.

I walk toward him slowly, looking around as though observing the scenery in his made-up world. I stop in my tracks and look down. "Whoa, where'd that come from? There's an egg over here." And knowing what comes next in this game, I add, "I wonder if it will hatch soon."

"You have to watch me hatch."

"I'm watching."

He starts squirming around and unfurling. "You have to guess what I'm going to be."

It's always T-Rex, but I have to be wrong first or he gets mad. "A duck," I say.

"Nope!"

"An ostrich."

"Nope!" his hands come out, fingers curled menacingly. "I have sharp claws."

"Hmm... are you a carnivore?"

"Yup!" He gets up on his knees, elbows tight to his chest, hands out and curled with their claws. Then he roars and gets up on his feet.

"T-Rex!" I say.

He lets out a big roar and stomps toward me. I fall over and curl up, and he pretends to eat my head.

Dad swoops down, picks Ben up, flies him through the air, and lands him on his feet again. "Go get dressed, kiddo," he says, and Ben stomps like a T-Rex all the way to his room.

He comes out with a new change of clothes in hand and proceeds to strip naked in the living room as Dad plops down in the recliner, watching him with a smile. Mom hums a song as she does dishes in the kitchen. Some nursery rhyme tune. The Valium has kicked in.

Ben holds up his shirt and shows me. "Mom got me this new shirt. See, it gots dinosaurs on it."

I lock eyes with Dad a second. I look back to Ben.

"Hey, buddy," I say. "You're getting to be a big boy. Maybe you should change in your room now."

Blood Gravity

Dad scoots forward in his seat. "He's just a kid." He grabs Ben around the waist, taking him into his lap and tickling him. He adds, "And this is family."

Ben falls to the floor, and Dad gets up, lifts him in the air and flies him naked around the room. Then Dad sets him back down and smacks his butt.

I watch Ben's face closely, looking for signs of worry, embarrassment, fear, any hint that Dad makes him uncomfortable, but I don't see it. There's nothing there but simple, five-year-old innocence.

Sometimes I wonder if I'm worrying for no reason. If what happened between me and Dad was just between me and Dad and not an indication of a larger propensity for what the outside world would consider immoral behavior.

The outside world. Somehow we all live in a bubble separate from that in this house. I look at Dad's face and feel guilty for being bothered by it at all. It's not like I ever told him no. And I'm sitting here in this house just like he is, like Mom is, like Ben is—like there's nothing wrong. Except my chest is tight again, my muscles are tight. Dad's gravity is a black hole, and I'm not sure I want to be around him today.

I look away into the kitchen as Ben gets dressed, at his drawings of all the trees on the fridge.

"Hey, Benny," I say. "What's the biggest tree you've ever seen?"

He thinks a moment and then spreads his arms as far apart as they go. "Maybe this big," he says.

"You ever see one wider than a car?"

"Wider than a car?" His voice goes high-pitched in disbelief.

Gayle Towell

"There's a place in California with redwood trees that big, and bigger."

"Whoa," he says.

"You want to drive down and see?"

"That's a six-hour drive," Dad says.

"I know," I say. "Can I take him? We'll stop overnight and come back tomorrow."

"We could all go," Dad says. "I haven't seen you in a few weeks. I was planning on catching up this weekend."

"It's been a while since I've done anything just me and him," I say. "It could be a brothers trip. You and Mom can have the rest of the weekend to yourselves. When was the last time you had that?"

Ben runs up and hops into my lap, landing a knee in my gut, making me wince. He looks at Dad. "Please? Can I go?"

Dad looks to Mom in the kitchen.

"It's fine with me," she says, with medicated bliss. "I think it would be good for him."

"Pleeeease!" Ben begs Dad.

Dad sighs. "Fine. But we'll have to do something together soon," he says. "I expect a call when you get there."

CHAPTER TWO

Not more than an hour after we leave, Benny starts squirming in the back seat, saying, "I really need to go potty."

"Already?" I say.

"Really bad," he says.

"Can you hold it for like ten minutes?"

"I'll try," he says and proceeds to make this whimpery whiny noise the whole way. I step on the gas, keeping my eyes peeled for the next rest stop. Seven miles down the road, I follow blue signs to an exit and park the car.

"Still dry?" I ask.

"Yeah," he says, unbuckling.

I walk him to the restroom, the whole while he grabs his crotch in despair, then he says, "I can go in by myself."

"I'm not letting you go in by yourself."

"Mom lets me go in by myself."

"It's not safe."

"Why?"

"Let's go, and we'll talk about it back in the car, all right?"

I open the door for him and follow him inside. The floor is sticky, and the whole place smells like sweat and piss. We're the only people, but I stand guard, my back to him as he uses the urinal.

Back in the car as soon as we pull out of the parking lot, he says, "How come it's not safe?"

"What?"

"The potty," he says.

"Because there might be strangers in there."

"Mom already telled me about strangers. I don't talk to strangers."

"It's *told*, not *telled*. You need to listen to Mom about the baby talk," I say. "And it's not the talking to strangers I'm worried about."

"Are you scared I'll get kidnapped? But if you're outside the door they wouldn't get away."

"That's not it," I say.

"Then what?"

"Sometimes..." I sigh. "Sometimes, some people try to hurt kids."

"Like hit them or something?"

"Or something," I say. "So, anyway, point is—you're too little to go in there alone."

"Mom lets me," he says again.

* * *

Blood Gravity

As we near Eugene, Benny recognizes this stretch of road from when he's visited me at college, and he shouts out, "Can we stop and see the ducks?"

"Sure," I say.

"And then the playground?"

"For a little bit, I suppose."

I pull into the parking lot at a park with a series of duck ponds and walking paths. It's overcast out, and a little chilly, but overall not bad weather for April.

Not long after we're out of the car, Ben shouts, "I want to touch the sun!"

"What?" I say. He points at the large, scale model of the sun by the side of the main pond. "Oh." I follow as he runs over and smacks at it with his hands. It's a good foot taller than he is.

"Don't get any ideas," I say. "We don't have time to see all the planets." Scale models of the planets are also spread out through the park—all the way to Pluto which is a three-and-a-half-mile hike.

His attention quickly turns to the waterfowl. He runs right up to the edge of the main pond and reaches into his jacket pocket, pulling out a handful of crumbled animal crackers and tossing them into the water. In no time, more than a dozen ducks and geese gather around, fighting over the crumbs. He takes a few steps back, reaches into his pocket and throws a few more crumbs out on the ground. The birds come ashore, gobbling them up and hissing at each other. Benny shakes his pockets out onto the ground, and the birds are right up on him, some of them nearly as tall as he is, wanting more.

"Jake, help!" he says, and I scoop him up before he gets pecked to death, setting him on my shoulders. I hold onto his legs,

and he wraps his hands around my forehead.
"Those are some hungry birds!" he says.
"No joke," I say and start walking toward the playground.
"Dad says birds are dinosaurs."
"They're related to dinosaurs," I say. "Dinosaurs are extinct."
"Why?"
"I don't know. An asteroid or something."
"And it exploded and they all died?"
"Yeah."
"Where did it come from?"
"Space."
"Why?"
"It just did."

We cross a bridge over the rushing, dirty waters of the Willamette River, then go under an overpass and the loud rushing sound of cars overhead, then along a path uphill from the river. We're passed by bicyclists ringing their bells.

"There's a man sleeping down there," Ben says and points downhill into the brush at a man in multiple layers of dirty clothes sleeping on cardboard.

"Yeah, there is," I say.
"Why?"
"Because that's where he sleeps."
"Is he dangerous?"
"Don't know," I say.
"He's a stranger," Ben says.
"Yes."
"I won't go potty if I see him in there," he says.
"You don't need to go again already, do you?"

"Not yet." He sucks in a deep breath and squeals, "A other planet!"

We're passing another scale model. "That's Jupiter," I say. "We must have made it through the asteroid belt unscathed."

"What?"

"Nothing."

As soon as he spots the playground, he practically leaps off my shoulders, and I nearly drop him onto the concrete. "Careful!" I say.

He gets his feet under him and runs straight toward the play equipment. I have to jog to keep up.

There are dozens of kids and parents running all over. I keep a steady orbit around the edge of the playground, avoiding the crowd and trying to track Ben as he runs up a rock wall, slides down a slide, leaps off a bridge. I don't know how he's so happy and comfortable with all the chaos and noise. Maybe I was like that at his age, too, but now it's just disorienting and unsettling. It's as if each person exerts some aura of variability. They could be happy, sad, judgmental, or any number of things all at once. They're all sharp and hyperreal.

The playground is huge and has a giant sand play area where you can dig down and find replicas of dinosaur fossils, which Ben does and drags me over to make a guess as to what each one is. I identify a dead-a-saurus and a crumpledactyl. There's a stage coach, an old-west village, and all sorts of stuff to climb on.

Ben hops on a swing, and I watch his face. His smile reminds me of Mom, except her smile is plastic half the time. Valium-induced. He's somehow learned to copy it. But he seems to be having fun. I start making comparisons between him and the other children. Do they look equally as happy? Are there any fundamental differences in their body language or apprehensions? Is Ben normal? Would I be able to spot which kids aren't?

A little girl in a blue dress who looks a few years older than Ben sits on her knees in the grass, poking angrily at the ground with a stick. Is it just kid-play, or something else? Did I look like that as a kid? Is her home life normal? Maybe everyone has secrets and so they all look the same.

The little girl looks up at me staring, her eyebrows coming together like she's suspicious, so I turn to find Ben again.

Except he's not on the swing anymore.

I scan the playground and start circling, not worried at until after I've made a full orbit and not seen any sign of him.

I start walking through, entering the chaos, the noise filling up my head, looking in all the play equipment, calling his name. "Benny!"

My heart is in full sprint when I finally find him running back over from a water fountain at the far end.

I grab him by the shoulder. "You need to stay where I can see you!"

His eyes get big, and his cheeks blush.

"I was calling your name," I say. "Didn't you hear me?"

"I was just getting water," he says. "I thought you were watching."

I sigh. "It's fine. You just scared me is all. We should probably get going. We've got a long drive, still."

"I don't want to go."

"Come on, Ben. I told you we could only stop for a little bit. It's already been more than that."

He folds his arms, stomps his foot, and says, "No!"

"You want to just go back home, or do you want to go see

the redwoods?"

His eyes go sideways, and he bolts for the playground equipment again. I run after him, catch him, and sling him over my shoulder. But as I try to leave, he starts screaming, "Put me down! Put me down!" and all the mothers look over at me like I'm a child abductor.

"Goddammit, Ben!" I set him on the ground, my hands tight on his shoulders to keep him in place as I kneel in front of him. "Are you a baby or a big kid?"

"Big kid."

"You're not acting like one."

His eyes well and redden. His mouth opens as he starts crying.

"Shh," I say. "It's no big deal, all right?"

But he just cries louder.

I wipe the tears off his cheek with my thumb. "Come on, Benny. You're fine. Let's get some lunch. What do you want for lunch?"

He sniffs and looks like he's thinking for a moment. "Can we get ice cream for lunch?"

"As long as you don't tell Mom."

His smile returns, and I hold his hand, leading him back to the car.

After a meal of ice cream, we hit the road again, checking into a motel when we get to California.

No sooner do we get into our room than Ben uses the bathroom with the door wide open. When he comes out, he says, "Can I take a bath? Please?"

"You know how to do it yourself?"

"Can you help me?"

"I'll show you," I say.

I walk him into the bathroom, and he loses all of his clothes along the way. He steps into the tub, and I show him how to turn the water on and change the temperature.

"When you get it the right temperature, pull the stopper up to plug the drain so the tub will fill," I say. "Turn it off when there's enough water, and push the stopper down when you're all done to drain it." I get him soap and a washcloth, lay out a towel, and leave him in there, closing the door. As he soaks, I turn on the TV and click through the channels, settling on some news broadcast. After a while Ben comes out, wrapped in a towel, then runs around drying off, tosses the towel aside and jumps naked on the bed.

"Get your PJs on," I say.

He lands on his seat and slides off the bed, then digs through his backpack and gets dressed. I turn the TV off.

"Come here a second," I say. "I need to talk to you about something."

"What?" he says.

"Just come here."

"Are you mad?"

"Mad about what?"

"Was I being a baby like at the playground?"

"No. That's not it at all. I'm not mad at you about anything. I just want to talk. Come sit."

He sits crisscross on the bed, facing me. I study his face while he waits, and I try to determine what my words should be. I'm trying to remember how I viewed the world at his age. I'm trying to remember where things went wrong years later, and if there was some missing piece of information that if someone just planted in my head early enough would have led to better decision making and understanding of right and wrong. Then I hear Dad saying, *Morals vary greatly among different societies and cultures.* He says, *Sometimes we just have to trust our instincts.* If I think about it too long I'm going to forget why it's all wrong. Dad's trained me well enough I could make an argument in support of anything.

"What?" Ben says.

I watch his freckled face a moment, wondering what Dad sees when he looks at him. "You know what privates are, right?" I say.

He giggles. "Yes."

"You know why they're called privates?"

He shakes his head.

"Because they're supposed to be private—that means other people can't see them. That's why people wear clothes and cover them up and stuff. No one—absolutely no one should see them except you, right?" I cringe because Dad would say, *That's a really naïve point of view, now, isn't it?*

"You saw them," Ben says.

"I shouldn't ever see them either unless you need help with something. But you're a big boy now, right? You don't need help with things. You know how to take your own bath and clean yourself and get dressed."

He nods.

"So no one should see them."

"Not even Mom and Dad?"

"Not even Mom and Dad."

"The doctor looked," he says.

Exactly, Dad would say. *Bodies are natural.*

"Well, doctors just have to check to make sure you're growing right. But no one else, not ever. Okay?"

"Okay," he says, looking down into his lap like he's disappointed.

"What's wrong?" I say.

"Is that why I can't go potty in places? Will people try to see?"

All boys and men have the same parts. Nothing to be ashamed of.

"There's something else I need to tell you and you need to listen, all right?"

He nods.

"It's not just strangers. Sometimes even people you know—they can do bad things."

Touch is part of love.

"Like what?" he says.

"Like lots of things. But that's why I said—even Mom and Dad—no one needs to ever see your privates."

"Except doctors," he says.

"Yeah. But you need to start getting dressed with the door closed. You lock the bathroom door when you go potty, and you can take baths by yourself now, right?"

"Okay."

"It's really important," I say.

"Why?" he says.

"It just is." *You know this is all a line of bullshit, Jacob.* "And if anyone tries to see you or touch you, you have to tell someone, okay? Doesn't matter who tries it or what they say, you tell another adult. You can call me, okay?"

"Okay," he says.

"Promise?" I say.

"Promise," he says. "I can tell Dad or Mom."

My face is hot. I take a deep breath. "Remember what I said about how sometimes people you know can do bad things?" He nods.

"If it's ever someone you know, tell me. Okay?"

He nods, but he looks confused. I can't breathe right. My eyes start to burn.

"What's wrong?" he says.

"Nothing," I whisper. "I just don't want anyone to hurt you."

Hurt? Dad would say.

I start to feel like I'm floating. My skin is buzzing, and a fist is wrapped tight around my throat.

"Don't worry," Ben says, smiling the plastic smile he learned from Mom. "No one will do that."

I look away, open my mouth and try to take a few careful breaths to make the feeling go away. If Dad heard all I said, he would get that look of disgust he gets when I've done something wrong. He'd tell me I wasn't using my head and got these ideas from TV or something. *Everything is a spectrum. Only idiots think in black and white.*

"Can I watch cartoons?" Ben says.

"Uh... it's really late," I say. "We want to get up and see the big trees tomorrow, right?"

"Please?" he says.

"Fine. Just for a little bit."

"Yay!"

I find Ren & Stimpy for him, and then lock myself in the bathroom.

Gayle Towell

The ache in my chest won't leave. There's too much in my head, and there's only one way I know to make it stop.

My hands shake as I pull my pocket knife out, flip it open and lift my shirt, exposing my collection of scars. I unbutton my jeans and slip them down past my left hip, trace my hipbone with my fingers until a spot feels right, then I put the blade there and saw and press until the skin gives way to bright red. My head clears as I mop up all the blood with my fingers, wiping it away until it stops. I don't know why this works. It just does

I hold the red there in my hand until it dries, then I rinse my hands and the blade in the sink.

I look at my red eyes in the mirror and whisper, "Fuck you, Dad. Fuck you, Dad. Fuck you, Dad," until he's out of my head.

* * *

The next morning we're hiking through the redwoods.

"Holy moly!" Ben says as he tries to wrap his arms around a tree. But it's like trying to hug a mountain.

"Holy moly!" he says again. "Look at that one!" He skips ahead.

I don't know if it's the trees or the fresh air or what, but there's a sense of freedom in being here. Just me and Ben with no Dad hovering over everything. I wonder, for a moment, if I will ever be a dad. Down in my gut I know there's too much in the way for that to ever happen, but I decide I don't care right now.

I tell Ben, "You know some of these trees are over a thousand years old?"

"Are they from dinosaur times?"

"No, dinosaurs were way before that."

"They're so big!" he says.

"Look up," I say. "See how tall they are?"

He steps back and looks up trying to see the top of the tree. Then he looks all around, worried.

"Jake?" he says.

"What?"

"What if one falls? Will we die?"

He comes back over to me and grabs the bottom of my jacket tight in his fist.

"You'd hear it, you'd see it coming, and there would be plenty of time to get out of the way."

"But they're so big," he says. "I can't run very fast."

"I can," I say. "And I'd carry you with me."

As we continue on, he keeps a tight hold on my jacket, tugging me at an odd rhythm causing me to nearly trip over him every few steps.

"Come here," I say, holding my arms out. I lift him up so he's sitting on my shoulders.

* * *

After spending all morning in the redwoods, we stop for lunch and begin the drive home. Ben sleeps most of the way.

Mom has dinner ready when we get there, but it's late, and I still need to drive back to campus and study for 8:00 a.m. class tomorrow. So she sends me off with a sandwich.

Ben follows me out to my car. I squat and tell him, "Remember what we talked about, right?"

He whispers, "You mean about privates."

Gayle Towell

I nod. "Call me, okay?"

He nods. I hug him, get in my car and wave goodbye as I pull out of the driveway.

I remember when I first left home for college feeling a sort of relief, like I had been committing a criminal act for so long and keeping it under wraps, and then I finally walk out of the room, leaving the misdeed behind. Maybe I got away with it. Maybe no one would ever have to find out.

At the same time, it's still with me, and not just because of my fear for Ben. There's a sick confusion of missing when I'm away from home. Like maybe I'm scared that Dad's the only person who could love me.

I still remember how it all started. I was ten, and I asked Dad about sex jokes I heard at school one day. His explanations led to secret hands-on demonstrations and feeling extra special. I was over the goddamn moon for a short while, before he took it further and further and further. It only stopped when I moved out.

Maybe Benny will never ask. Maybe Dad won't try it again. Maybe I'm worrying over nothing. Maybe it was just me.

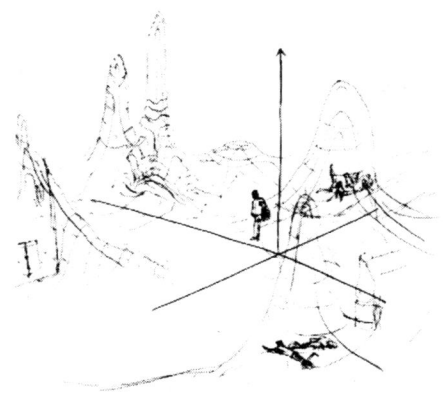

CHAPTER THREE

The anxiety is always worst on Mondays. Coming off the weekend, it takes a day to get used to sitting in classrooms again without feeling like my heart is going to explode. It starts when I wake in the morning as an overwhelming desire to stay in bed. The day looms over me like this insurmountable thing. I could go through my schedule minute by minute in my head and fail to identify a single thing that would justify it, but that feeling is there anyway.

My roommate Koa thinks he's my alarm clock, thinks I don't know when to wake up. But I've been awake for half an hour already, listening to him typing on his computer when 7:30 rolls around, and he sings his stupid song he made up just for me. "Wake-up Ja-cob, wakey, wakey, wake-up."

"That really isn't necessary," I say.

"Sure it is," he says. "You know you like it."

Gravity presses me into my mattress. Blankets lie heavy on

Gayle Towell

top of me, keeping me secured in a safety zone. But with each passing minute, the moment when I absolutely need to exit my sanctuary gets closer, and a stale nausea starts to wrestle with my stomach.

A granola bar hits me on the head, thrown by Koa. "Your scrawny ass isn't skipping breakfast again," he says.

I sit up and let the granola bar fall to the floor.

As I dig clothes out of my dresser, Koa starts telling me about the basketball team's latest victory. I ignore him and disappear into the closet to change in private. When I reemerge, I find him stuffing the granola bar in the front pocket of my backpack.

"Thanks," I say, slip on my shoes, grab the backpack, and head out the door.

I drop the granola bar in the first garbage can I pass.

Part of the problem is I can't tell where norms are. Dad spent so many years filling my head with this broad spectrum of human behaviors and unorthodox ways of thinking that I'm bound to say something stupid if prompted. *What do you think of the weather today?* someone will ask. And I'll answer, *Here? Or in Saudi Arabia?*

My multivariable calculus homework from last night is swirling around in my head. I imagine a function representing my anxiety. A scalar field spread across campus. The maxima of the function will be at the locations where large groups of people congregate, and the minima in the dead spots—like behind a dumpster. My total anxiety is then the integral of this function over the path I walk to class, and I must choose a path which minimizes this total. I mentally assign anxiety values out of a scale of one to ten to the different locations. The cafeteria is a ten. Most doorways are seven or eight. But these numbers fluctuate because people fluctuate. Maybe I should take statistical mechanics next fall.

In class I sit in the back near the door like always and let myself get lost in the symbols. There's something comforting about mathematics. The pure objectivity, maybe. There's a sense of control. An indisputable right answer.

Today we're learning about conservative vector fields. Gravitational fields are conservative vector fields. What's special about them is their line integrals are independent of path. You could take a direct path from point A to point B, and the result is the same as if you meandered all over the place on your way. It only depends on where you start and where you end. The journey is entirely irrelevant.

In psychology class, again I sit in the back near the door. The only difference is Rachel, a junior with red-brown hair pulled back in a ponytail. She says, "Hi" as she takes the seat next to me. We sometimes study together, and she likes to talk before class starts.

"How was your weekend?" she says. "You went home, right?"

"Took my kid brother to the redwoods."

"Aw, I'm jealous," she says. "I've always wanted to go there."

"It's just past the border in California," I say. "Less than a four-hour drive from here. You could be there and back in a day if you had a car."

"Unfortunately, I don't have a car," she says. "I'd have to convince someone to go with me and give me a ride."

I nod and look down at my notebook. After a pause, I say, "So... how was your weekend?"

Gayle Towell

"Went for a bike ride Saturday, but that was about it," she says.

Professor Martin walks in the room and everyone quiets down. Rachel and I open our notebooks as the professor starts writing on the whiteboard.

The topic for the day is something called gaslighting. As Professor Martin describes, it's a form of mental manipulation in which someone either intentionally or otherwise presents false information, making the other person doubt their own perceptions and sanity. She says the term comes from an old movie called *Gas Light* where a guy dims the gaslights in the house, and then flat out denies it when his wife notices the changes, and she eventually believes she's crazy.

I start thinking about Dad and the forever-old question of right and wrong and who wanted what and whose idea it was. The stories he'd tell of different cultures and civilizations. In some places a nine-year-old bride is fine. In ancient Greece, the practice of pederasty—an older man engaging in a romantic relationship with a boy for education purposes—was simply normal. And those stories are all fact; they're all true. Dad never presented false information.

Professor Martin says, "It can come in the form of denial that things occurred. Or it could be a manipulation of blame. If someone frequently blames their unhappiness on the behavior of another, then the other person may come to believe this alternate reality where everything is their fault. Or, if someone tells you something is normal, but you feel deep down that it isn't or that it's wrong, this might be the result of gaslighting."

That last line—the word "normal" and the word "wrong"—it cuts something inside of me. Like someone just detached my spleen. A burning sense of being offended starts to well up. I don't know if it's my own anger, or if I'm channeling Dad's offense at those words, but I want to reject this topic like my survival depends on it. I almost never talk in class, but I somehow need to say something. I have to make this go away. My hand shoots up, and I say, "What do you mean by wrong? Who defines wrong?"

Everyone in the room turns to look at me. The professor's eyebrows come together like she's almost concerned more than curious about my question. Then she says, "When it hurts, I suppose. It's wrong when it hurts."

Hurts. That word hangs over my head like a terrifying vulnerability and makes the anger fall through the floor. A single syllable that feels like a sob or a lurching heartbeat when said out loud. My face burns hot, and it feels like my skin is vibrating.

The professor continues the lecture and everyone faces forward again. I avoid looking up, instead picking at the binding of my notebook with one hand and trying to copy everything she says verbatim with my other. I try to make my breaths even, but I feel like I'm suffocating.

"The gaslighter's presentation of the world is what you accept as your reality because any time you protest, you are ignored, or ridiculed, or otherwise given indication that you're out of line," she says. "Often, when under the influence of this behavior, it is difficult for the victim to even see it. Victims will constantly second guess themselves, feel crazy or overly sensitive, are always apologizing, feel depressed or unhappy, frequently make excuses for someone else's behavior, or withhold information from others so they don't have to make excuses. They don't trust their own judgment."

Gayle Towell

Then we're all told to take a moment and try to think of an example of gaslighting that we've encountered in our lives or seen on TV or in a movie.

I run through the list of signs, and it all feels so familiar. But I keep telling myself—Dad always told true stories.

I'm missing something. The "hurt" part.

You hurt me, Dad.

What? One eyebrow would go up, and his lip would snarl in disgust. *If I hurt you, you say something when it happens. If someone feeds you chocolate ice cream for years, all the while you preferred vanilla, that's on you.*

He'd tell me anyone could be considered a gaslighter if you twist the facts enough. He'd tell me about confirmation bias, and I'd agree with him.

I think about how he always tells Mom she worries too much and plies her with Valium. That's always felt wrong. But just as I'm about to write it down, I start to see all of the ways in which Mom does worry too much. So that can't be an example. Or can it?

I look up at the words "Tells you something is normal when you feel deep down that it isn't" on the board, right below "Gaslighting: Manipulating someone's perception of reality." My stomach is floating, and all the edges of my body are on fire. I want out of this room so bad, but I force myself to stay. I have to stay. I have to be a good student.

The instructor asks for volunteers to share their answers with the class. Still I've got nothing, so I just listen as different students tell what they wrote in turn, all the while Dad's voice in my head deconstructs their words until they're nothing. They're all wrong.

But we're all supposed to expand on what we wrote and

Blood Gravity

turn in a two-page paper on Friday.

Rachel looks over and says, "What did you write?"

I turn my empty notebook page toward her. She shows me a full page of writing. "Looks like I got a head start," she smiles. "You want to trade papers again? Maybe by Wednesday night?"

"Um..." I tap my pencil on the desk. "Sure."

"I'll email you," she says.

* * *

After uneventful honors history and literature classes, I'm in my dorm room in the afternoon drafting out the psychology paper, when Koa appears, sweating from the gym. Nearly every day he plays basketball there with a group of friends. I've joined him a few times, but it never took. I was the only non-Hawaiian.

I'm sitting on my bed, scribbling in a notebook as he invades the room with the stench of armpit.

"What you working on there?" he says.

"Psychology paper."

"You want to help me with my physics later?"

"Maybe if you shower."

"What, you don't like my musk?" He walks over, lifts his arms, and tries to move an armpit toward my face, but I kick him away.

"Fine, I'll shower," he says. "Just for you."

He leaves the room, comes back twenty minutes later smelling like soap. Then he flops on his bed with his physics homework.

"What are you working on?" I say.

"Biot-Savart law," he says.

"Never heard of it."

"Me neither," he says. "Do you know how to do line integrals?"

"Bring it here."

He plops his books in front of me. I show him how to make the right substitutions and set up the integral, and then he pokes around trying to perform the integration, sighing frequently and intentionally.

Finally I say, "Integration by parts?"

"And that's why you're a genius," he says and starts working it out. When he finds success, he says, "You should take physics."

"I don't want to take physics."

"But you'd be good at it."

"Doesn't mean I want to do it. Besides, I had Astronomy last year."

"So what's the paper about?" he asks.

"Gaslighting."

"What's that?"

"A way of labeling the actions and motives of others."

"Can I get one more integral out of you, then I'll leave you alone?"

"Aren't engineering majors supposed to be able to do math all by themselves? I'm not going to be there one day when you design a bridge."

"I'll take that as a no," he says. "You need to relax. Psych is a non-majors survey course. No one expects anything more from you than complete sentences and basic punctuation."

He goes quiet, lost in his homework, and I stay buried in mine.

The whole while I write the paper, I feel like I'm making it all up. I am distorting reality in order to make a case for gaslighting. While part of me wants to write some sort of manifesto about the ambiguity of the term, my need to maintain my GPA trumps all. Curiously, both desires arise from a want to please my father. He would approve of me disagreeing that he gaslights to the point of deconstructing the term entirely. He would also approve of me getting an A. And since he won't ever see my paper, but he will see my grades, I go with the latter.

I title it "The Worrier." And I change the names to protect the innocent. Or guilty.

* * *

The Worrier

Mrs. Jones is a worrier. This is fact if you ask her husband. Just this last weekend she worried when her son came home later than he said he would. She was also worrying about her younger son—the five-year-old—and the fact that he wets the bed. She worries that sucking his thumb will hurt his teeth.

She worries if her children don't eat right, if one of them gets sick. She worries when they get hurt. She worries so much about everything that there is a rule in her house—don't upset your mother. It became universally understood that she was fragile and unbalanced. She overreacts.

Her children accept this without question. If their mother used that word—"worry"—it wasn't to be taken seriously. In order not to "upset" her, they'd sometimes need to go along with her worry, appease her in the same way you might appease a child begging you to look under his bed for a monster.

When her youngest son got sick with the flu when he was three and ran a fever of 103, she worried, took him to the doctor, came home with instructions to give him Tylenol, and Mr. Jones said, "See? I told you it was nothing to worry about."

It was always nothing to worry about and always no big deal. But it seemed like she worried all the time anyway. Her husband even convinced her she needed prescription medication to "calm her nerves." So to this day, any time that word "worry" comes up, she takes a Valium.

She will never argue, never accuse her husband of wrongdoing, never entertain for a second the thought that he is less than ideal, because he has convinced her any thoughts of that nature are a result of her irrationality or her nerves.

Mrs. Jones no longer trusts her own emotional reactions. She is utterly convinced that she needs the medication, that she is unstable, and that her husband only points all this out to her out of care. She doesn't know who she is if he doesn't tell her.

But the thing is, taking a toddler with a high fever to the doctor is recommended by the American Academy of Pediatrics. A high fever could be a sign of a secondary infection and require antibiotics. Her son could have become dehydrated or had a febrile seizure if it got worse. Previously healthy children have died from the flu.

Thumb sucking has been shown in studies to contribute to overbites when continued past toddlerhood. The five-year-old will start getting adult teeth soon and this habit could mean braces in the future, or a deformed palate. And that's beside the fact that prolonged thumb-sucking, as well as the bedwetting, are both signs of anxiety.

Blood Gravity

Mrs. Jones's worries are almost always valid if looked at objectively. If anything, she should worry. It's important for her wellbeing and the wellbeing of her children.

What her husband is doing is an example of gaslighting—manipulating someone else's reality to the point where they don't trust their own judgment and think they're crazy.

* * *

But I could just as easily demonstrate how Mrs. Jones does worry too much when you compare the statistical likelihood of her feared outcomes to the odds of getting a concussion while playing basketball, or getting food poisoning from a home-cooked meal.

The paper is only a page and a half and not the two pages required, but I send it to Rachel as is. She in turn sends me hers—a far more interesting piece on the relationship between gaslighting and sociopaths.

When I see her in class Thursday morning, we discuss our papers briefly, and she says, "You never actually get into why Mr. Jones gaslights his wife. Like, is there some ulterior motive? Does he cheat on her? Lie? What?"

She stares at me like she wants me to answer that right on the spot. When I don't, she adds, "But that could give you the half page you're missing, anyway. Other than that, it's good as always."

Before submitting the paper in class the following day, I make up some bullshit about how the husband does this because he doesn't want his wife to worry about when he comes home late because he's cheating on her. It hits the two page mark on the nose.

After class Rachel says, "A bunch of people are getting together tonight at my cousin's house off campus. Nothing too

Gayle Towell

outrageous, but it should be fun. Do you want to come?"

"I'm not really much for parties," I say. "Or crowds in general."

"Don't think of it as a party. It's more of a gathering. Come on—I can meet you outside your dorm and we can walk over. It's only like a mile."

She stares expectantly, her eyebrows up as high as they can go.

Against my better judgment, I finally say, "Sure. Why not?"

"Awesome," she says. "I'll meet you at seven."

CHAPTER FOUR

At a quarter till seven it occurs to me maybe I should make some effort and at least wear a nice shirt. I dig through my dresser, discarding one after another.

Koa lounges on his bed, watching. He says, "You going out?"

"Just a house party thing," I say. "A girl from one of my classes invited me."

"Like as a date?"

I freeze, trying to remember exactly what Rachel said in case I misinterpreted. "I don't think so. She just said there was a party and I should come. That's not a date, is it?"

He shrugs. "Maybe not officially, but that might be where she's headed." He points at my stack of shirts. "The green one," he says. "Makes you look hot."

"Hot?"

He laughs, then sits upright. "Oh my god. You've never been on a date before, have you?"

"It isn't a date," I say.

"Why do you think she invited you?"

"As a friend? Because we study together sometimes?"

"Dude, she likes you." His face is all bright and excited.

"As a friend," I say.

"What are you so scared of?"

I go into the closet, close the door, and change into the green shirt.

When I come out, Koa says, "I'm just going to assume you have, like, three nipples or something. You're the only dude I know scared to change his shirt in front of anyone."

I ignore him and find my shoes.

"You'll be fine, man. Just be yourself," he says.

Rachel is waiting just outside my dorm building, texting someone when I come out. She looks up. "You ready?"

I nod, and that same anxiety that always hits when I go to class on Monday starts welling up inside, making my chest hurt.

"You okay?" she says. "You look pale."

"I'm fine." I try to smile.

As we walk, she tells me about her cousin whose house we're going to. The cousin's name is Aubrey and used to babysit Rachel when she was little. The cousin lives in a house with three roommates, all graduate students. Rachel doesn't know how many people will be there, but they've bought a lot of beer.

It's a cream-colored house with a small yard. The grass is mown, but peppered with weeds. There are maybe a dozen people there when we show up. Rachel introduces me to Aubrey, who has the same hair color as Rachel, but is taller and bears no other resemblance. I'm introduced to a few more people, and soon Rachel and I have plastic cups of keg beer in our hands.

It occurs to me this is the first beer I've ever been handed by someone other than Dad. I drink it down in the hopes of numbing the anxiety.

More people come, and soon the place is crowded and loud. I somehow lose track of Rachel and just sort of stand awkwardly, changing my location by a few steps any time it looks like someone might strike up a conversation. I think about multivariable calculus again and minimizing my path integral. I'm pretty sure this is not a conservative field.

After a few more beers and time wandering in the haze of people, Rachel finds me again and we sit on a couch. Techno music starts down in the basement below us.

"You look like you're thinking," she says. "What about?"

"There's a lot of people here," I say.

"That's usually how these things work."

I take another swallow of beer. "Your paper was really good," I say. I don't know why I bring it up. Maybe it's the intoxication. I feel nothing, but am not sure that's a good thing. "I wouldn't have thought to compare gaslighters to sociopaths."

"It makes sense, though, right?" she says. "Anyone doing that intentionally is at least partially sociopathic."

"What do you do about it?" I say. "Someone who's being gaslighted. What do they do?"

"Did you zone that part of the lecture?"

"Must have."

"Well, you remove yourself from the gaslighter's sphere of influence."

I laugh.

"What?" she says.

"Nothing's ever that simple. If it was so easy to leave, then no one would ever get themselves deep in a situation like that in the first place."

"What do you know about it, son of Mrs. Jones?" she smiles.

I suppose changing the names in my paper was a rather thin veiling, but she could at least pretend. Without a word, I get up and fetch more beer.

Rachel follows. "Did I offend you?" she says as I swallow half the cup down.

"My dad's not a sociopath."

"I didn't mean—"

I shake my head. "All of psychology is so arbitrary that if you wiped all present knowledge of it from everyone's memory and made them start over from scratch it would look entirely different. It's a soft science. You know for over two thousand years—dating back to the time of Hippocrates—it was thought that women's emotional problems were the result of disturbances of the uterus. That's where the word 'hysterical' comes from. And even in the last century we have Freud and his crackpot ideas—all those things your subconscious mind is supposedly doing. Oedipus complexes. Dream interpretation."

She places her hand on my forearm. I stop talking and just stare at her fingers.

"Come with me downstairs," she says.

We walk downstairs, the whole time her hand stays on my arm. I drink the rest of my beer.

The music throbs as people dance in a big open area. Dozens of people everywhere, laughing and talking mixed in with the music. The smell of sweat and beer. Rachel's hand still on my arm, trying to pull me into the middle of it all. But my chest hurts even through the intoxication.

"I don't dance. I can't dance," I stammer.

She turns my way. "Come on. Let yourself go a little and have fun."

I'm too busy trying to breathe properly to protest, and she tugs my arm, pulling me deep into the moving mass of people. Everything is bright flashes, a wind tunnel of noise, and nothing stands still. I become dizzy, looking all around. Rachel lets go of my arm and moves with the crowd in front of me. I lock eyes with her. "I-I think I need to go," I say.

"What?" she shouts through the noise.

I lean close, my mouth near her ear where I can smell her shampoo, like fruit and coconut.

"What?" she says again.

"I need to go," I say.

"Oh, there's a restroom upstairs. I'll show you," she says.

"No, I mean I need to leave."

"Why?"

I walk through the crowd, unsteady from the beer. She follows me up the stairs where it's quieter, and as I make it to the front door, she says, "What's going on?"

"I'm not good with crowds," I say. "I'm not feeling well."

She stares at me with a look of complete and utter disappointment. "Want me to walk back with you?"

I shake my head. "I just need some air."

She keeps staring.

I mutter, "Sorry," and head out the door. It's starting to rain.

Gayle Towell

Walking fast into the night, my head clears a little more with each step. The weight of the crowd and the noise evaporates. I go to the river and walk the path alongside it, sobering up as the rain grows heavier and the night grows colder.

CHAPTER FIVE

The following Monday, I feel out of place sitting next to Rachel in psychology class. But she doesn't say anything about Friday night. She doesn't say much of anything at all.

In the evening Dad calls, asking how things are going. "Still getting A's?" he says.

"Mostly."

"Mostly?"

"School's fine."

"That's what I like to hear," he says. "So listen—it's supposed to be really nice weather this weekend. It's been forever since we've gone camping. What do you say?"

"Uh..." I close my eyes and pinch the bridge of my nose. I love camping and being out miles from anywhere. Peace and quiet. Space to think. But I'd rather not go with Dad. "I've got midterms coming up," I say.

"Just for the weekend," he says.

"Maybe... maybe some other time, Dad. Sorry."

"Fine, then. It'll just be me and your brother."

After the phone call ends, I follow Koa to the dining hall and sit at a table with him and all of his friends from Hawaii, listening to them joke and talk and complain about professors. But I can't stop thinking about Dad going camping alone with Ben.

So after dinner I call him back and tell him I'll come along after all.

* * *

After class on Friday, Dad comes by with Ben to pick me up and head out to the forest southwest of Mt. Hood.

Ben hands me a drawing he made. A tent in the woods. And a dinosaur. Nothing disconcerting.

"Nice," I say.

The whole drive there, Ben chatters away in the back seat, telling me new words he can spell, commenting on the scenery and how the trees here, despite being over a hundred feet tall, are tiny since seeing the redwoods, and on and on, and are we there yet?

It's almost seven when we park at the trail head. Dad and I do the heavy lifting, hauling the backpacks on our backs, and Ben skips along the trail in front of us. It got up into the seventies today, and the setting sun is warm through the gaps in the trees. The earthy smells of pine, dirt, and sap combine with the sounds of birds singing spring songs and insects buzzing.

Ben stops, crouches and crawls towards some bushes, fishing animal crackers out of his pocket and holding them out. He tosses them lightly as Dad and I catch up to him.

"There's chipmunks," he whispers, and we hear them rustling in the brush.

"Come on up," Dad says. "We want to set up camp before it gets too dark."

We keep hiking, the trail never level for long, always going up and down. We come upon a clearing—a hillside in full bloom with wildflowers. Blues and yellows and pinks. And beyond them, Mt. Hood looms large and snowcapped in the clear blue sky. Dad stops to snap a few pictures.

"Can I pick some?" Ben asks.

"Just one," Dad says. "You're supposed to leave nature alone. This is a national forest."

Ben plucks a pink flower and says, "I'm saving it for Mom."

"Don't know how well it will last the weekend," I say. "Maybe we can press it flat and try to save it that way."

The sun isn't more than a few fingers above the horizon when we settle on a spot to set up camp. We get the tent pitched and start a fire with the bundle of wood we packed in and some kindling gathered from the forest. As the flame grows brighter, the sky grows darker, and I shave pointed ends onto sticks for roasting hot dogs. Dad pulls out a six pack of beer, hands me one and takes one for himself.

Ben says, "Can I have one, too?"

"You're too little," I say. "You're supposed to be twenty-one."

"You're not twenty-one," he says.

"I'm close enough." I spear a hot dog with a stick and hand it to him. "Here. Go hold that over the fire, but be careful."

After Ben eats half a hot dog, he begs for marshmallows.

Gayle Towell

He goes through half a bag, roasting them, sometimes catching them on fire, eating the charcoal results anyway, until his hands and face are covered in sticky mess. Dad pulls out a package of baby wipes and cleans him up.

The fire dies down. Dad and I have polished off the rest of the beer. We get out flashlights, but Ben keeps one hand grabbing Dad's belt loop, thumb in his mouth, afraid of getting lost in the dark.

"Think it's time to settle in for the night," Dad says.

After Ben panics over a spider, we get our sleeping bags laid out, Dad between me and Ben. It's starting to get cold. Dad tickles Ben. He asks him if he's warm enough. They whisper. I tap Dad on the shoulder. He turns my way.

"It's late," I say. "Should let him sleep."

"I need to go pee," Ben says.

I sit up. "I'll take him."

I hold Ben's hand and the flashlight and lead him to a tree. "Go ahead," I tell him, and turn around to offer him privacy.

"I'm scared," he says.

"I'm right here," I say.

He finishes, and on the walk back I say, "You need to try and get you some sleep or you'll be too tired to have fun tomorrow."

"I had to pee," he says.

"I know. That's done."

Back in the tent I make sure the kid gets zipped up tight in his sleeping bag, no access points. I lay back down and Dad rolls towards Ben and rubs him vigorously all over through the sleeping bag to warm him up.

"I think he's good, Dad," I say He kisses Ben on the

forehead, then focuses his attention my way.

"So what have you been learning in school?" he says.

"Lots of things," I say.

"Like?"

"I don't know, um, in math—multivariable calc. We're doing line integrals."

"You're way beyond me in that," he says. "Might as well be speaking a foreign language."

"Alexander the Great in history class," I say.

"Alexander the Third of Macedon," he says. "You know by the time he was thirty he created one of the largest empires of the ancient world?"

I laugh. "And then he was dead two years later."

"Is that right?"

"He supposedly got sick and died. They think it might have been poisoning."

"There was a lot of that sort of thing back then. You know that's where the tradition of clinking glasses before drinking came from? Guests would pour a little of their drink into the host's cup. The host drank it to prove he didn't slip them any poison."

"I heard that was a myth."

"Really? So why do people clink their glasses then?"

"I don't know."

"I'm pretty sure I'm right," he says. After a moment of silence passes, he picks the conversation back up with, "You know Alexander was tutored by Aristotle?"

Ben drifts off to sleep, thumb in his mouth as Dad and I continue comparing notes about Greek history by the light of a flashlight. And it's actually kind of nice. Or maybe it's the beer. But I've always liked history and it's in a large part because of talks like this. It makes the world feel so big—not only is there a whole globe full of seven billion people, but add a temporal dimension and there are so many stories.

"God, I've missed these talks," Dad says. "I've missed you, kid. You know it? How's college besides class? You don't have a girlfriend yet, do you?"

"No," I say. "Never know how to go about that."

"You've got time," he says. "You'll figure it out when the moment's right. Bet it's hard trying to find time to whack off with a roommate though, isn't it?"

He elbows me, grinning.

Then he leans in closer and whispers in my ear. "Benny's snoring. You hear that?"

We wait a moment in silence, listening to Benny's light breathing. Deep in satisfied sleep.

"Cute, isn't it?" Dad says. "Reminds me of you at that age." He grins again, then reaches his hands down into my sleeping bag and up under my shirt on my stomach. They're ice cold. He snickers as I squirm. "Come on now," he says. "You don't want your old man to get frostbite."

"Goddamn that's cold!" I whisper.

"Shh," he says. "Don't wake your brother."

His hands stay on me, and I stop squirming as they warm up. Then fingers slide down under my waistband.

"Now there's warm," he says.

"Dad..." I say. His gravity is too strong. I'm getting sucked in again. The black hole. Why didn't I see this coming?

"What? Maybe I should warm my hands on your brother. How fast do you think he'd shoot awake if I froze him?"

"He's sleeping. Let him sleep," I say.

Blood Gravity

"You're not," he says. His fingers start exploring, caressing their way down into my pubic hair. The physical feeling is one of calm and comfort, but I know where this is leading and I know I should tell him to stop.

But I don't. And I don't know why I don't.

He finds my dick, his fingers move across it, and against my will it starts to swell. "Been a while, hasn't it?" he says.

I say nothing, do nothing, just lay there letting his hands move over me, and as much as my brain wants to fight it, it all feels good. And this was so normal not that long ago. Asking him to stop would lead to an argument he'd most likely win. Or he'll wait until I'm asleep and his hands might find their way into Benny's sleeping bag.

So I let it happen. He unzips his sleeping bag and mine so that they open toward each other. My pants and underwear are shoved down and his hands are all over me, one reaching around back, a finger in my crack. His pants come down, and he grabs my hand and puts it on his hot, sweaty crotch, his breathing becomes heavy with approval. "God, I've missed this," he says, his breath in my ear, warm against the cold air. "You know how much I love you?" My eyes burn, but I don't know if I'm scared or just overwhelmed.

Soon he's lying on top of me, kissing my neck, pushing my legs apart with his knees, his hard cock pressing below my nut sack. My hard cock pressing into his stomach. He spits on his hand and rubs himself, then presses his dick head against my asshole, pushing harder, harder until it gives way.

I knew it would hurt, but I wasn't prepared for how much. Insufficient lubrication coupled with not having done this for a while makes it feel like he's ripping me open. He doesn't ease up, just keeps pushing himself deeper. I'm gasping for breath, and his hand goes over my mouth to muffle an involuntary whine. My eyes water, it hurts so bad.

He breathes in my ear, whispers, "Don't wake your brother. Just relax. You're rock hard. This can't be all bad."

Once he's all the way in, I feel as if I've been impaled. I know he's making me bleed again. He's always laughed at the blood. Made some joke about how it's like a girl losing her cherry. Telling me I'll get to see that for myself someday. He always made it sound like I was earning a badge.

He snickers in my ear. "Losing your cherry again, aren't you?"

He pulls back slowly, then pushes back in. His hand still covers my mouth. He kisses the corner of my eye where a tear rolls down. His hand comes off my mouth. "How's that?" he says.

I don't answer. He pulls back and then rams himself up hard into me and repeats. I grab part of my sleeping bag tight in my fists. My insides are on fire. I try to take deep breaths, but my body is forced to inhale and exhale at the rate he's ramming me. I try to relax, try to wait it out. I know it'll get better soon. It'll get numb.

Beyond the light of the flashlight half buried in Dad's sleeping bag I can see the shadow of Ben sleeping. He isn't moving, just slow, up-and-down breathing. I stare at him, waiting, ready to put a stop to this the second he wakes up.

The ground beneath me is uneven and stabs at my back in places. My left hip is bent in a way that's making my leg tingle. Everything in the middle of me is a confused mix of pain and pleasure. I've been trained since before puberty to get off on this.

I try to put my mind elsewhere. I think about Alexander the Great, poisoned and dead at 32. I run through the Greek alphabet. *Alpha, beta, gamma, delta....*

With a final grunt, Dad finishes and collapses on top of me. But then he whispers, "Your turn, or it isn't fair."

He moves down, puts his mouth on my dick, and I have to focus because he won't let this go. He won't stop until I finish, too. So I sink into it, let it feel good. His thumb goes up my sore ass, finds my prostate, and I give it up, squirting into his mouth.

For a brief moment, the surge of oxytocin that comes with release makes me feel like this is all okay. He loves me; I love him. But as the rush fades, I sink back into my body, feeling shredded and ruined, like my very core has been twisted into something no one can ever see, no one can ever want. I want to burn it all out of me, but it just stays and festers and soaks all the way through.

Dad fishes the package of baby wipes out of his backpack and we wipe ourselves down, but the real dirt is all on the inside.

"God, I needed that," he whispers and kisses me on the forehead. "You better?"

I nod.

"I'm proud of you," he says, shuts off the flashlight, and drifts off to sleep.

I lie on my back, staring up into the complete darkness of the tent, my body warm and throbbing in my sleeping bag, my face cold in the night air. The air laced with the smell of trees and sex and sweat. I lie absolutely still, letting the nebulous darkness make my whole body go away until I am completely numb and dead inside.

The darkness fills my head until I'm lost in its abyss. I fall asleep, but don't dream.

***

I wake in the morning to Benny poking his fingers in my ear while making sounds like a buzzing mosquito.

He smiles when I look up at him. He looks so happy.

"Dad's making breakfast," he says. "We're going on a hike!"

I sit up and pain shoots right through the middle of me. "Go on out," I say, gritting my teeth. "Let me get dressed."

He leaps out of the tent like some cougar, and I hear him laughing and talking to Dad as I peek under my sleeping bag and find my underwear bloodied. I find the baby wipes, try to clean myself better, dig out fresh clothes and get dressed.

I step out of the tent, and Dad smiles at me, cooking pancakes on a pan over a fire. "Morning," he says.

My gut cramps. "I need to piss," I say and wander off into the brush. I drop to my knees by a tree and throw up. I kick dirt over the vomit and sit out there awhile, shaky and weak.

Benny's only five. Thirteen more years before he's old enough to move out. I'll be thirty-three by then. Thirteen more years I have to keep Dad off him.

Dad comes through the brush looking for me. "You okay?" he says.

"Fine," I say.

"I've got breakfast ready." He reaches into a pocket, pulls out a pill bottle and shakes one into his palm and hands it to me. "Vicodin," he says. "In case... you know."

I close my fingers around the pill. "Can I talk to you about something?" I say.

"Sure, but make it quick."

"If I hadn't come on this trip and it was just you and

Ben..."

"What?" he says.

"Benny's too little," I whisper.

"Too little for what, exactly?"

"You know," I say. "Last night?"

"Jesus, Jacob, what do you take me for? I'd never do anything with your brother he didn't ask for. We've never done anything you didn't ask for."

I nod.

"There's no way you're upset about last night, as hard as you came." He grins and pats my shoulder. "Come on, let's go eat."

I follow him back to the campsite, dropping the pill into the dirt on my way, but can't stomach much food. After breakfast we pack up a small backpack for a day's hike. Dad takes the burden of hauling it.

I may be sore, but in some ways it's welcome. I feel like I need to hurt. If anything, I want to hurt more. Walking puts me in a trance like a baby being rocked. Nothing feels real.

The hike takes us mostly uphill. Dad keeps trying to talk to me. "How far do you want to hike out today?" he says.

"Don't care," I say.

"Have you given any thought about what you're doing this summer?"

"No."

"I can help you look into getting an internship somewhere."

"Sure."

"I wonder what your mother's doing with the house all to herself this weekend."

Gayle Towell

"Worrying," I say.

He laughs. "Ain't that the truth?"

He grows tired of my one-word answers and turns his attention to Ben, pointing out the different types of birds and explaining again how they're related to dinosaurs. He talks about how different birds live in different parts of the world.

After the excitement of finding a patch of dirty snow in the shade, Ben says he's tired of hiking and asks to ride on my shoulders.

"Can't today," I say. I look Dad in the eye.

Ben turns to Dad. Dad shoots me a grimace of disapproval, hands me the backpack, and scoops Ben up, setting him on his shoulders.

Dad's hands on the kid's legs.

Benny straddling the old man's head.

Maybe Dad will cop a feel. Maybe his fingers will walk up the kid's legs until his thumbs get to the good spot. And I'll just pretend like I don't notice because there's not a goddamn thing I can do about it. If I tell him not to, he'll deny anything happened. If I somehow get the balls to report it, there would still be no goddamn evidence. Just his word against mine.

As for what he did with me, not reporting it is—as it always was—a foregone conclusion. I didn't say no. I didn't fight it. I did nothing.

I am twenty goddamn years old, and I did nothing.

So maybe I can't care anymore.

When night comes, I stay out by the dying fire as Dad and Ben settle in the tent. I listen for any and every sound. They talk a little. The flashlight light moves around and shadow puppets project on the side of the tent. Then the light goes out and it's

Blood Gravity

silent. I wait awhile longer, then go in, shining a flashlight on them. They're both sound asleep, both in their respective sleeping bags, but Dad has his arm around the kid. Benny's got his thumb in his mouth. I stare at him a long while before going to bed myself, watching his face for any sign of anything. But he just looks peaceful. Like a baby. He's still a baby.

CHAPTER SIX

I make it through class on Monday without feeling much of anything. In the evening, sitting on my bed in my dorm room, in the middle of multivariable calculus homework, Dad calls.

"You have a good Monday?" he says.

"Yeah," I say. Koa sits at the desk, typing at his computer. I stare at the back of his head. Dad's loud enough on the phone that the whole conversation can be heard.

"I think my back is ruined from sleeping on the ground all weekend," Dad says. "I'm getting old."

"Yeah."

"You boys had fun, though."

"I have a lot of homework to catch up on," I say.

"Right," he says. "How's the studying going for midterms?"

The expected answer is "good," but I don't say it right

away. I'm holding my breath and tensing.

"Midterms?" he repeats.

"Good," I say.

"That's what I like to hear." Those words pour over me like thick syrup. He has coated me with his approval again in a way that doesn't wash off.

"I should..." I take a deep breath. "I should get back to studying."

"Well," he says. "You let me know how things go later this week, right?"

"Yeah."

After hanging up, it becomes impossible to focus. My eyes go over the words and symbols in the textbook, but none of it goes into my head. There's no room for it. It might as well be hieroglyphs. I press my pencil into my notebook until it breaks.

Koa says, "Was that your dad?"

When I don't answer, he adds a sarcastic, "Okay, then."

My skin buzzes all over, and I want to rip it off. A sharp scratching, something cutting into me, breaking through it, letting the blood out, the sting of it, anything to take away the crawling contamination feeling. It's all I can think about. Stab something into my rib cage. Shave a slice of skin off my forearm. But Koa is here, sitting at the desk, pecking away at his computer, affording me no privacy. There isn't even enough space to have thoughts in here.

Finally he gets up. "I'm heading to the cafeteria. Join me."

I shake my head. "Not hungry."

"Not hungry? Your skinny ass needs some meat."

"I need to get this work done by tomorrow."

"Fine," he says. "I'll bring you back a potato or

something."

As soon as the door clicks shut I dig my pocket knife out of my dresser. I pull the window blinds down, sit on my bed, and lift my shirt. I go for the gut—right below my belly button, where Dad's hands reached first in the tent, freezing me. I hold the skin taut with one hand and then press and saw with the blade until it gives way—pink flesh at first, then red blood. I run the knife a little deeper. Blood rolls down in fat drops, and I catch it in my hand.

And just then, the door opens. I turn and see Koa staring at me. "What the...?" he says.

I look down and cover my new wound with my hand, still holding the knife with the other. "I... uh... just dropped my pocket knife," I say.

He waits as if trying to piece together how that could even happen. Then he says. "I thought you were doing homework. Why do you have a knife?" When I don't answer, he adds. "Do you need to go to the health center?"

"I thought you went to dinner," I say.

"I forgot my ID." He looks to his desk, finds his wallet and pockets it. "Seriously, though—what happened?"

"Nothing. Just a scratch."

His face furrows in concern. He says, "I'll be back after dinner," and leaves.

"*Fuck,*" I whisper to myself, tossing the knife on the floor and finding a sock to mop the blood. I lie back on my bed, touching the cut with my finger and making it sting.

I remember being thirteen or fourteen the first time I ever did this. I thought I'd invented it. I used my fingernails and scratched at my forearms one night when I couldn't sleep. I scratched and scratched, deeper and deeper. It took me somewhere else, and I didn't want to ever stop. The skin was raw and open, and it stung against my bed sheets all night.

In the morning when I woke up, the marks had started to darken and scab. I had no explanation for them, and Mom was knocking on my door telling me to get ready for school. I just sat on the edge of my bed, staring at the scratches until she pushed the door open.

"What on earth happened to your arms?" she said.

Dad came in the room behind her, staring at me, one eyebrow raised, lip snarled in disgust. Mom looked to him and then to me.

Dad said, "Did you do that?"

Mom said, "Why the heck would you do something like that?" But she couldn't look me in the eye with Dad standing right there, and there was a weakness in her voice.

Dad locked eyes with me, and I knew full well it didn't matter what I said. Any words that came out of my mouth, he'd twist them around until they became what he wanted them to be. If I fought the twisting, he'd lay on the disapproval. And his disapproval felt like a death sentence. He was a boat, and life was an ocean. If he threw me overboard, there'd for sure be sharks.

When I didn't answer, Mom folded her arms and said, "Only crazy people do that, Jacob. Unless you want to end up locked in a nut house, it better not happen again."

So I hid it better after that. I'm sure Dad still noticed, but he never once said anything.

I pick at the cut on my stomach, tear it, make it bigger, dig my fingernail in. Then I slide down to the floor and find the knife again. I pull my pants down to my knees and start cutting at my thighs. I rub the blood all over and into my skin. I get lost in it, just digging and digging at my own flesh, and it burns and hurts. I fantasize about digging out muscle fibers and finding my way to the bone. I claw at the cuts and scratch them harder where they burn, and when I finally slow down I realize I've made one hell of a mess. Nothing that needs stitches—I was careful enough for that. Mostly just meaty surface wounds. I have no idea how much time has passed. Koa might be back at any moment.

I need a shower. I press the sock against the wounds until they stop dripping, and then pull my pants back up, grab a towel and a change of clothes and head to the bathrooms. I make it into a shower stall without seeing anyone. As the blood runs off my body under the hot spray, every new nick stings. And yet I'm wishing I brought the knife in with me. I imagine slicing off my dick and nuts, putting them in a box and sending them to Dad. *Here you go, Dad. Yours forever. I don't fucking need them.*

After drying off, I press the towel against the wounds again to make sure there isn't much bleeding, then I get dressed. When I return to my room, Koa is back from dinner. He's standing in the middle of the room, looking me right in the eye, holding the bloody knife out like it's a dirty rag.

"This is sick, man," he says. The usual humor in his voice is completely gone. "I know exactly what this is. My sister does this shit."

I grab it from him and toss my blood-stained towel on top of my bloody socks.

"You've got blood on everything."

Someone comes down the hall. I turn around. It's the RA. He comes into our room, looks at Koa.

Koa says, "That's the knife," pointing to my hand. Obviously the RA's appearance is no coincidence.

Blood Gravity

"It's a pocket knife," I say, folding it closed.

The RA puts his hand out. "Can I see it?"

"Why?"

"You know you aren't allowed knives with blades longer than three inches."

"It isn't," I lie. The scrutiny feels like being surrounded by bees.

He sighs and puts his hands on his hips. "Jake, can I get you to come to my room a minute so we can talk?"

"About what?"

"Please?"

I look at Koa, but he avoids eye contact. Then I follow the RA downstairs. The wounds stick to my clothes, and I wonder if any of it will soak through. I don't want to look down and see. I try to let my t-shirt hang loose in front of me. We go into his room. I sit on the small couch, and he sits across from me on his chair.

"Can I see the knife?" he says.

I hand it to him. He opens it, then handles it carefully after seeing the blood on the blade. He sets it on the coffee table. "You know that's longer than three inches."

"It's just a pocket knife," I say.

"Yeah, and what were you doing with it?"

"Nothing, I just... I dropped it when I had it open and accidentally cut myself."

"Accidentally? Look, the knife's getting confiscated, but that's not my main concern here."

"What do you mean?"

"Your roommate tells me you've been out of sorts ever since getting back from the weekend. He says you seem distracted and depressed, and he's worried."

"There's nothing to worry about."

"Did something happen? What's going on?"

"Nothing." I wonder for a moment what would happen if I fessed up. Would they kick me out of school? Lock me in a nut house? They'd probably lock me there forever if they found out what really goes on in my head. I'd tell them about Ancient Greece. I'd tell them about the Melanesian Tribes of New Guinea. I'd tell them anything so they wouldn't look at me like I was just too stupid.

"Are classes going okay?" he says.

"They're fine."

"Are you having problems with friends? With a girlfriend?"

I shake my head.

"Family?"

That word feels the same as "hurt." It carries the same sensation of terrifying vulnerability.

"Is it something you want to talk about?"

"There's nothing to talk about." I feel so scared all of a sudden. I'm shaking. I try to tense all of my muscles to make it stop. If I'm found out, I'll lose everything.

"You know we've got counselors on campus. It's all confidential."

I shake my head. He leans forward, elbows on knees, cocks his head to the side and starts delivering a lecture about some kid who committed suicide in the dorms three years ago, and he takes concerns very seriously and on and on. All the while I stare at the dented wood trim on the edge of his coffee table, studying the lines and irregularities, wondering what part of the tree it's from, letting my eyes focus on the carpet, rendering the table blurry, then back again. Then I let everything go out of focus until strange things start appearing like in those magic eye puzzles.

Finally I say, "Are we done?"

"Yeah," he says. "But please give some thought to what I said, all right? And my door is always open."

I nod and leave.

My jaw is clenched tight as I head back up the stairs. I'm sweating, and my hands are still shaking. Koa is back on his computer at the desk when I return. I shut the lights off without asking, leaving him in the dark, save the glow of his computer screen. Then I say, "In the future I'd appreciate it if you'd mind your own fucking business," and crawl into bed, blankets pulled over my head before he can turn the lights back on.

"Not cool," he says. "Not cool. I think that's the first time I've ever heard you cuss." He waits like maybe he expects me to react. When I don't, he sighs and says, "I'm going to leave you alone right now, Jake. But you're my friend, all right? Whatever is going on, I can try to help if you just ask."

In a short while I hear him typing on his computer again. All of my new cuts sting and burn and stick to my clothes, but what hurts worse than anything is some phantom feeling in my gut—in my ass—like Dad just tore me all over again. Sharp, stabbing spasms that make my eyes water. I stay burrowed under my blankets so Koa can't see me. I stay perfectly still.

CHAPTER SEVEN

All night long I keep thinking I hear the door opening, and jolt awake, hyperventilating. Sometimes I hear Koa snoring, and I think it's Dad right next to me. It's always some weird combination of familiarity and fear. This sense of normalcy and comfort coupled with wanting to run away. Two in the morning it happens again, and I nearly fall out of bed. The light comes on, and Koa stands there rubbing his face, squinting.

"What the fuck, man?" he says. "Do you want some sleep aids or something?"

I get up, slip my shoes on, and grab my jacket.

"Where are you going?" he says.

"For a walk."

"You want company?"

"No." I brush past him on my way out the door.

The only sign of life is a campus police car doing patrol. I assign the car an anxiety function value of ten. Everything else is just a one or a two right now.

I avoid the headlights. The last thing I need is somebody pulling up and asking me what I'm doing out so late. At the edge of campus I cross a street and make my way to a footpath that goes over the river. I sit in the middle of the bridge and listen to the rushing water in the dark.

I look up at the sky, but it's cloudy. No stars. I wait there until I grow impatient, until all I want to do is pick at the cuts again, then I get up and walk along until I find the giant, yellow model sun next to the duck pond. I find Mercury, Venus, Earth, Mars all scattered about relatively close, then I follow the long path to Jupiter, Saturn, Uranus, and make it to Neptune as the real sun starts to brighten the horizon. Then I turn around and head back.

Koa says nothing to me as I get my books together to head to class, just sits in his bed, watching. I walk across a campus that is now filling up with people, level ten anxieties everywhere, my cuts stinging, my gut cramping. I take a seat in the back of the math classroom, pull my textbook and notebook out of my backpack and plop them on the desk. I can hear my heartbeat up in my ears. The whole room looks distorted. The professor walks in, and everyone starts passing their homework forward, but I never got mine done. I manage to make it through lecture in a state of dissociation, then I march like a zombie to psychology class.

Rachel takes one look at me, scrunches her face up, and says, "You okay?"

"Fine," I say, but it's weak.

"No, you're not." She waits for me to say something else.

"Maybe I'm coming down with something."

"Then go back to your dorm. I'll bring you the notes

later."

"I'm fine," I say again.

Professor Martin walks in with a stack of papers to hand back.

Our gaslighting papers.

Rachel gets hers first. A bright green A circled at the top. When I'm handed mine, she says, "What did you get?"

Likewise, I have a green circled A.

"Awesome," she says.

How'd you do on your paper, son?

I got an A, Dad.

That's what I like to hear.

A tight knot grows in the center of my chest. The professor writes on the board, but she seems so far away, and I can't make my eyes focus. It's as if my entire body has become my heart, the whole thing contracting with each beat. I look to the door, but my legs are numb. Then that sharp stabbing pain is back in my ass. I grip the edge of my desk. I can't even breathe until it wanes. But it comes right back, and my eyes are burning. Rachel keeps glancing sideways at me. I'm going to pass out if I don't leave. I manage to get to my feet, knocking my notebook off the desk in the process. Everyone watches as I stumble out of the room.

I disappear into a bathroom and lock myself in a stall just as another wave of excruciating ass pain hits.

I sit on the toilet, leaned sideways with my head against the stall wall, my mouth open wide in a silent scream, scared to make a sound. I don't want anyone to know I'm in here. No one can know what's going on.

Soon I'm trembling uncontrollably, terrified my heart's going to give out, my body's going to break. My face is wet with sweat. I can't get enough air. The pain keeps coming in waves until it's all I know. This becomes my whole world, all hidden away in a bathroom stall.

Enough time passes that the pain finally eases, and I come back to Earth, aware of my surroundings. I no longer feel quite like I'm dying.

I wait a while longer before getting out of the stall and splashing water on my face at the sink. I don't even go back to collect my things from the classroom. I just walk as fast as I can back to the dorm. Just my luck the RA is in the common room. I know I look like crap, and I'm already on his worry-radar. He pops up as soon as he sees me and steps right into my path.

"Everything okay?" He puts his damn hand on my shoulder.

"Don't fucking touch me," I say, the words coming out without planning or thought as I flinch away from him.

His hands go up, attesting innocence. "Whoa, chill out. What's going on?"

I don't say another word, just jog up the stairs to my room and close the door. Koa's gone. He has class straight through until noon, and it's only eleven. I open my bottom dresser drawer before remembering the knife was confiscated. I grab the hair at the back of my head tight in a fist and pace around trying to find an alternative. I settle on nail clippers, sit in bed, lift my shirt and start clipping bits of already damaged skin off, bleeding deep, red blood down my belly, soaking into the waistband of my underwear. And the impulse grows and grows in my head. I don't want to stop this, ever. I want to rip my whole body apart. I'd cut off my own limbs if I had the tools to do it right now. I punch myself hard in the thigh, making my leg go dead.

I surprise myself by sucking in air like someone drowning. The sound seems foreign. I dig my fingers into the new cuts and tear at them, get blood deep under my nails again. I reach into my pants and start squeezing the life out of my dick, just strangling the fucker. If I grip it tight enough for long enough, it'll go dead and fall off. The rest of my blood can then drain out of the stub that's left. I twist it and pull it until the pain is all-consuming. I'm going to do it. I'm going to fucking rip my own dick off.

But there's a knock on the door. My grip loosens, and I heave a few deep breaths before screaming, "Leave me the fuck alone!" in some guttural, strangled voice like a subterranean troll who's been angered by a trespasser.

The deep voice on the other side of the door says, "This is campus security. I'd just like to talk to you for a minute."

"Just a sec," I say, but I'm still actively bleeding. I cut deep. I pull my hands out of my pants, and go into a new panic, trying to rub the blood off my fingers and change my shirt because it's a mess now, too. I throw the nail clippers under the bed.

I open the door to let him in, and then sit hunched on the bed, hiding the evidence of my midsection.

"Jacob?" he says.

I nod.

He sits on Koa's bed, facing me. "We got a call from your RA. He's concerned for your safety. I need to ask a few questions to make sure you're okay."

I shrug. "I'm fine. I don't understand what the problem is."

"Have you been having any suicidal thoughts recently?"

I shake my head.

"Have you thought about hurting yourself in any way? I understand a knife was confiscated yesterday?"

"No, I uh... it was just a pocket knife."

He nods and looks away. "All right. Well I want to let you know about the counseling services available on campus." He pulls a card out of his pocket, then scribbles something on the back of it. "And this is a crisis hotline number." He hands me the card. "Completely confidential. Just want you to be safe."

I nod. "Thanks, but I'm fine."

The officer stands up. "Well, hang on to that," he points at the card. "Just in case, all right?"

I nod, and he leaves. As soon as he's gone I crumple the card and toss it in the trash. I take a shower to clean myself up, then try to bandage the cuts with what few Band-Aids I have left in my dresser.

I have to get out of here.

After getting my luggage out of the closet, I start packing everything I care to keep because maybe I won't even come back. Then I start to wonder if I should bother packing anything at all, because maybe I won't need anything where I'm going.

Koa comes back from class in the middle of this process and says, "What are you doing?"

"Don't worry about it," I say.

"Seriously, man. What the hell happened?"

"Drop it," I say.

"You left. You went camping, right? You come back. You hardly say a word, and you're losing your shit."

I ignore him and just keep packing.

"Where exactly are you going?" he says.

"Doesn't matter."

CHAPTER EIGHT

I start out headed south, but the drive reminds me of the trip to the redwoods with Ben. Part of me wants to hate him, to not have to think about him or care about him ever again. He's the whole reason I went on the damn camping trip. But I just can't. And now I don't know what to do.

I remember what Rachel said about getting outside the gaslighter's sphere of influence. If Dad is a force like gravity, then he reaches on forever, though with diminishing strength. Ultimately there is no escaping.

The solar system model spread throughout the park near campus is a one to a billion scale of the real thing. In reality, Pluto is 40 Astronomical Units from the sun. In the model it amounted to 3.5 miles. The heliopause is around 120 AU. So I've already left the solar system at ten miles from campus.

Then there's the Oort cloud—a cloud of frozen objects

surrounding the solar system extending out some 50,000 AU. 50,000 divided by 120 is... 400 or so. Since 120 AU was ten miles, then on the scale model I'd leave the Oort cloud after driving 4,000 miles. I'd need to leave the country.

If I wanted to make it to the nearest star, I'd have to drive a tenth of the way to the moon.

Swinging eastward after a while, I end up circling Crater Lake before the day is done. Always this feeling that the more miles I cover, the closer I will get to an answer. But what is there to find?

I pull off the side of the road near a hiking trail, get out and lean against my car awhile, staring at the trailhead. It'll be dark soon, but I start the hike anyway. Up and up and up as the sun drops lower and lower until it's gone. I stop at the edge of a cliff and sit in the moonlight staring down at a hundred-foot drop onto rocks below, wondering if this is what I've been trying to find all day.

Lifting my shirt, I pick at all of the cuts with my fingernails. Scratching and bleeding, and burning and bleeding. When I grow tired of that, I find a stone on the ground next to me, toss it over the cliff and listen to it clack and bounce. I want to fall. I want to drop so hard I splatter, shatter, break into a million pieces. I want to be ripped open. I want it so bad tears start running down my cheeks.

Then my phone rings. Somehow out here on this cliff I'm getting an excellent cell phone signal.

It's Rachel. For whatever reason, I decide to answer.

"Hey," she says. "You never came back to class today."

She sounds so normal that my present neurological processes have to reorder themselves before I can determine a response. "I just... I went for a drive," I say.

"Yeah, I talked to your roommate when I dropped off your notebook, and he seemed kind of freaked out. I mean, there's rumors going around that you're suicidal."

"No," I say.

"No, you're not suicidal?"

Maybe I don't actually know the answer to that. But it isn't really death I want. It's escape. "Remember what you said about gaslighting?" I say. "How you have to remove yourself from the gaslighter's influence?"

"Yeah."

"And I said it's not that simple?"

"Yeah."

"If someone has you like that, they have everything you do. That's why it's not simple. Everything you want, everything you are. You have to give all of it up."

"You don't have to give everything up," she says. "You just have to give them up."

"You don't get it. It's all too connected."

"What exactly is this all about, anyway?" she says. "Where are you?"

In the sky there's a bright star not far from where the sun set. Except it's too bright to be a star. "I can see Venus," I say.

"What, are you on a spaceship?"

"No. It's just in the sky."

I hear her sigh on the other end. "People really are worried."

"It's fine," I say. "Everything's fine. I just went for a drive."

"Mind if I tell them all you're still alive?"

"Go ahead," I say.

"You want to talk?"

"No. Like I said—I'm fine."

"Why am I not convinced?" she says.

"I have to go now," I say.

"Be safe," she says. "And you can call whenever. I don't care what time it is."

"Yeah," I say, and hang up.

Now there's nothing but the sound of trees rustling, and a hoot owl in the distance. I'm still staring at Venus—the planet closest in size to Earth. In the grand scheme of things, it's hardly far away, but I can make it vanish by covering it with my thumb held at arm's length. It's so small.

Earth is so goddamn small.

I pick up a stick and fling it end over end out into the cold, black nothing. It hits the rocks below. I find another stick and throw it. And another and another. I start hurling fistfuls of forest floor out into the open space of the night. I yell one big, loud roar, echoing off the hillside, absorbed into the trees. I yell again, but my voice gives out. My throat is raw.

Something is trying to break free out of my chest. Some big balloon in there expanding and expanding and rising up my throat. It bursts. I burst. I start crying, sobbing, unable to stop. It comes out forcefully, ripping me open.

I fight my way out of my jacket and shirt, exposing my entire upper half to the April midnight, just to feel my own body. To own it. I lie on my back in the cold dirt, staring up at the stars through blurry eyes. I spread my arms out to the side, and let the earth steal the air from my lungs until the crying wanes.

The chill hurts every bone, leaves every muscle in spasm. I roll onto my side, face pressed against the forest floor. My breath turns the dirt into mud, and it sticks to my cheek. I am outside of my body, unable to get air, the black night coming in patches and flashes of brighter grays.

"Fuck you, Dad. Fuck you, Dad," I whisper.

I sprawl out, hugging the earth, clinging to its cold carelessness. Floating around in some unreal space. Miles from anywhere. Alone.

Then my phone rings again, and it shocks me back into reality.

I let it keep ringing as I roll onto my back, wiping my face with my forearm. It goes to voicemail.

But it rings again. I look at who's calling and see my parents' number. They never call this late. I somehow know it's Ben even before I answer.

"What are you doing up so late?" I ask.

"I had a accident," he whispers. "But I'm not s'pose to upset Mom."

I pinch the bridge of my nose and take a deep breath. His voice feels like the word "hurt."

"I just need to know how to make the washing machine go," he says. "I already put everything in there. And I washed up by myself. With privacy."

"Look at you," I say, sitting back up. "You've almost got this. You're getting to be so big."

He lets out a small laugh. I talk him through adding the soap and starting the machine, then he asks, "Are you coming home this weekend?"

I stare down into the dark drop-off. "Benny... you know I'm proud of you, right?"

"Uh-huh," he says.

Blood Gravity

"And I love you. No matter what, right?"

"Are you coming? Pretty please?"

I take a deep breath and look up into the sky. "I'll try," I say. "I'll try."

After I tell him goodnight and hang up, I scoot a little closer to the edge. I throw another stick down into the chasm as hard as I can, listen to it smack against the rocks and break.

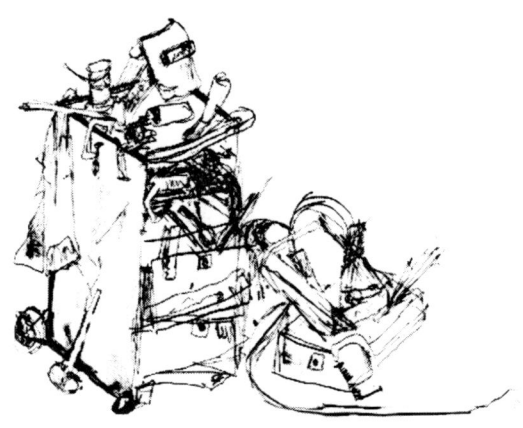

CHAPTER NINE

Warm, bright sun wakes me early in the morning after having spent the night on the cliff. I look down at the rocks below, squint, and imagine my body there. Who would find it? How would my parents be notified? What would they tell Ben? What would he think?

I keep hearing his voice from the phone call last night. *Pretty please?*

Caring about him hurts.

I can't remember what day it is. Wednesday? It must be Wednesday.

I could hike back to my car and drive back to school—pretend like nothing happened until people stop asking and leave me alone. I could answer Dad's phone calls, tell him what he likes to hear about how great things are and how well I'm doing in all of my classes. Go home for visits. Let him put his hand on my shoulder, grinning like he owns me. That syrup-thick feeling of him coating everything I do.

Except even entertaining that idea makes my hands shake. College is what Dad's wanted me to do ever since I could talk. And I sit in those classes, pushing through the anxiety, hurting and hurting for him, unable to stomach his disapproval.

He's why I tear at my body. He owns it, too, and I can't stand it. I want to rip it apart and ruin it. So he can't.

But if I leave school, then what? I can't go back home. I can't live in that house with that heavy air and him.

But I can't ditch Benny. I can't just check out.

I hike back, get in my car, and start driving, still going nowhere in particular. Sometime later, I stop at a rest stop to take a piss and wash my face. There are no paper towels or soap, just highly irregular water pressure. I splash my face with water and look in the dirty mirror. My eyes are bloodshot from crying, my hair is messed, my clothes are dirty.

A stall opens behind me, and I freeze when I see long, blonde hair in the mirror. And make-up. A woman's face. For a second I think I ended up in the wrong bathroom, but there are urinals along the wall. I just peed in one. She approaches the sink beside me and says, "The women's room was out of order," as she digs in her large, pink purse.

I just stand there, my face still wet and dripping. She locks eyes with me in the mirror and says, "You look like you've seen better days, kid."

I can't stop staring at her eyes in the mirror. Blue eyes, with coated, black eyelashes and blue eye shadow. She's older than me. Maybe by about a decade. "Where are you headed?" she says. She retrieves a hotel sample soap from her bag and unwraps it.

"Don't know," I say.

"Where are you coming from, then?" She turns the water on and begins washing her hands. Her fingernails are long, painted red.

"Uh... around," I say.

"You a vagrant?"

"No. Well... maybe at the moment."

"You're a runaway," she says. "How old are you? Fifteen? Sixteen?"

"Twenty," I say. She shuts off the water, and pulls a napkin out of her purse to dry her hands.

"I'd say you were lying, but a liar would pick eighteen. You've got the facial hair growth of a fifteen-year-old."

"I shaved a few days ago," I say, running my fingers along the minor stubble on my chin.

"Exactly," she says. She waves a hand at the small soap bar she left by the sink. "Soap's all yours," she says.

"Thanks," I say.

She digs in her purse again, produces a tube of lipstick, and with her face right up by the mirror, mouth open, she applies it. When she finishes she says, "Safe travels, Sport," and leaves.

I grab the soap and use it to wash my face and hands. I dry off with the bottom half of my shirt and head back out to my car.

I start the engine and am about to pull out when I see the woman from the restroom standing in front of a truck with the hood open, engine smoking. Hands on hips, she stares into it, disgusted. I turn my car back off and walk over.

"Do you need some help?" I ask.

"Got a new truck you can sell me?" she says. "I think this one's done for. You know anything about engines?"

"No, sorry," I say.

"I've called for a tow," she says. "But I need to get home tonight. I've got to be back at work in the morning."

"Where's home?" I ask.

"Hillsboro," she says.

"Oh." I suppose odds were great that she had to be from somewhere in the Portland metropolitan area. But my home town?

"Oh, what?" she says.

"I could give you a ride," I say.

"It's three hours away."

"I know," I say. "I'm from there. Or, I grew up there, I mean."

"You don't need to go out of your way," she says.

"I don't have a way at the moment."

"What's your name, Sport?"

"Jake."

She extends a hand to shake. "Savannah."

After Savannah's truck is towed away, we get in my car and hit the road. "So where are you coming from?" I ask.

"Bend," she says.

"What's in Bend?"

"A funeral."

"Oh, sorry."

"My dad," she says. "Cancer. We knew it was coming. Too many cigarettes. Do you smoke?"

"No."

"Good. Don't start." She slips her shoes off and rubs her feet. "What about your parents?" she says. "They live in Hillsboro?"

"Yeah."

"When was the last time you saw them?"

"Last weekend," I say.

"So what's your deal?" she says. "You look like you've been sleeping on the ground. But you've got a car and family nearby."

"Long story," I say.

"We've got a long drive," she says.

"I just... I don't know what I'm doing with my life right now. Anyway, I don't want to talk about it."

"It's a break-up, isn't it? Girlfriend dumped you?"

I shake my head.

"You're depressing me," she says, turns on the radio, and stares out the window.

A heavy ache settles into my chest again. I'm driving towards my hometown, pulled toward Dad again as if some comet approaching perihelion, burning, vaporizing. I always come back. At the same time I am thankful for Savannah. I at least have a clear goal for the next few hours of my life. This feels marginally better than floating.

Savannah alternates between silently staring out the window, to messing around with things in her purse, to randomly divulging details about people she knows. I don't talk much. I'm too spent. We make it to her house in the afternoon, and she invites me in.

Her house is painted white on the outside and most of the inside. Her shoes come off as soon as she enters, and she walks barefoot across plush carpet. I kick my shoes off as well. My socks are dirty. If she notices, she doesn't say anything.

"Sit." She waves at her sofa as she walks into her kitchen. "Can I get you some wine?"

"No thanks."

"Some water?"

"No thanks."

She fills a glass with ice water and sets it in front of me on the coffee table, pours wine for herself and takes a seat at the opposite end of the couch. Her feet go up on the table, crossed at the ankle.

"Do you really not have a home at the moment? You can't have been a nomad for long. Where were you before you hit the road?"

"The dorms where I went to school."

"You drop out?"

"No. Just... uh... something came up, and I had to leave."

"Were you failing?"

"No. Getting straight A's, actually."

"Did you get arrested? Cause some problem, and they kicked you out?"

"No. I left on my own."

"Were you involved in illegal activity? Are you running from something?"

"No."

"Couldn't afford it anymore?"

"No. Had a full scholarship."

"Then what the hell happened?"

I stare at the condensation forming on the glass of water and feel the sweat forming on my forehead. My chest hurts. My eyes start to burn and I don't know if it's anger I feel or weakness. I grab the glass and take a drink.

"Straight-A student, huh?" she says. "What was your major?"

Gayle Towell

"I hadn't declared yet. Was going to be History or Math."

"Math? You're a real brainiac, are you?"

I shrug. Now I miss school. I knew what I was there. I don't know what I am here. I take another drink of water, but there's that expanding balloon feeling in my throat and it comes on fast. I bite my fist trying to stifle a sob. "Can I use your restroom?" my voice cracks.

"Down the hall. First door on the left," she says.

I rush into the room, lock the door, hang over the sink, hyperventilate, tears dripping into the sink, then I vomit up the water I drank. I continue dry heaving for another five minutes until my gut muscles are sore.

I lift my shirt, looking at the scabbed mess in the mirror, and start picking at it. But I force myself to stop and splash water on my face instead.

When I come back out, Savannah looks at me, her eyes big, her mouth pursed. "Do you want to call your parents?"

I shake my head.

"What about friends? You have any in the area?"

I shake my head again.

"What's your plan? Where are you sleeping tonight?"

I shrug.

"In my experience," she says, "people without plans are usually without plans because they don't intend on sticking around in the world of the living." When I don't answer, she says, "Sit."

I sit on the couch and she disappears down the hall. She returns with a blanket and a pillow, plops them on the couch beside me, then goes into the bathroom and returns with a pill in her hand. She sets it next to the glass of water. "Take a Xanax and get some sleep."

Blood Gravity

I stare at the pill and think about Dad medicating Mom.

"You're a wreck, kid. Take the pill and lie down."

I do as she says, and she turns the lights off and closes the blinds.

* * *

I wake to a hand on my shoulder, shaking me. Savannah stands over me and says, "Good morning, Sunshine."

"What time is it?" I say.

"Six in the morning. You got a solid fifteen hours of sleep."

I slowly sit up, feeling rested, but not yet fully awake.

"I need to head to work," she says. "You're either coming with me, or moving along. I don't know you well enough to leave you alone in my house."

I end up choosing the former. Since her truck is still in the shop, I give her a ride. She directs me to a parking lot in an industrial area on the far side of town, in front of a building called Grove Machining.

Savannah is dressed in a short skirt, tight shirt, make-up, and high heels and we're walking into a machine shop.

We enter the front office. She clocks in.

"You work before?" she says.

"No. Just school."

She purses her lips. "Are you strong?"

"I can lift heavy things."

"Let me see your muscles."

"What?"

She holds up her own arms, flexing them to emphasize her point. "Your muscles."

Gayle Towell

I take my jacket off and flex my arms. She pinches my biceps.

"Stringy, but I suppose it'll do. Come on, I'll show you around the shop."

I follow her through a set of double doors into a large concrete-floored warehouse with dozens of heavy machines. Everything is dirty, and no one else is here yet.

"Look at this place," she says, her high heels clicking across the floor. "We've got scrap metal just lying in piles. We've got cabinets full of tools that have just been thrown in there. Not only does it make it impossible to find anything, but shit keeps getting broken. Are you good with organization?"

I nod.

"And cleaning? Getting shit squared away so no one maims themselves?"

"Yeah."

"All right, how about this?" She pulls open the drawers of a completely destroyed tool cart. "Think you can make this pretty by lunch time?"

"Um... I'll try," I say.

"I'll be in the front office if you need anything," she says. "The guys will be clocking in soon. Stay out of their way, and let them work."

After she disappears back through the double doors, I wheel the cart to a section of the shop that appears to be clear and proceed to empty everything out of the drawers, trying to organize tools by type as a handful of guys slowly make their way to the various stations around the shop. There is a considerable amount of garbage wedged into the drawers. I even find a half-eaten cheeseburger. As the shop fills with noise of drilling and cutting

Blood Gravity

and welding and shouting, I try to wipe the tool cart down as best as I can with a rag, then I clean each tool and designate which drawers they go in.

By lunch break I'm just finishing up. Savannah finds me and proceeds to open each drawer in turn, all the way to the bottom. Then she stands up, hands on hips. "You want a job here, you got one. We've been in need of a shop hand for some time."

"Um... okay."

"Follow." She turns around and starts walking away.

I follow her into the front office where she has a folded wad of newspaper—classified ads for apartments with one circled. She hands it to me. "Why don't you go check this out? I know the landlord. If he gives you any crap, tell him Savannah sent you. And go get you some steel-toed boots while you're at it."

I stare at the newspaper in my hands. "I don't—"

"You don't what?"

"I don't know if this is right," I say. "I'm not sure what I'm even doing."

"Exactly," she says. "So I'm telling you. If you come up with some better plan later, then go for it. Until then, you've got a job, and if you head to that address, you'll have an apartment."

"Okay."

"I'm keeping you busy, Sport. You'll thank me later. Shift starts at 6:30 a.m. tomorrow."

* * *

Soon I'm in a real estate office filling out a rental application for the apartment. I hand it to a man with a large gut and pit stains and wait while he looks it over.

"You've got no prior rental history?" he says.

"No."

"And your work history—job starts tomorrow?"

"Yeah."

"Where'd you work before that?"

"I was going to school before that," I say.

"You got anyone who can cosign?"

"No," I say.

"Get a cosigner and the apartment is yours."

"But, please. I don't have anyone. I need a place to stay."

"I can have a renter in this place by the end of the week with a more stable history. Why would I take a risk with you? Find a cosigner and it's yours."

"Savannah sent me," I say. "She says you know her? She said you'd be... understanding?"

"Savannah?" he says.

I nod.

"She sent you?"

I nod.

He lets out a long sigh and looks back over the application. "You got eleven hundred for first and last month's rent?"

All I've got is stipend money from my scholarship, but it's enough. "Yeah, I can cover that," I say. And I'll have little more than spare change left over for food until my first paycheck.

"Fine. Get me that in cash and the apartment is yours."

So I run to the bank, then back to the landlord's office, get the keys, and drive to my new place.

It's a dull gray three-story building with a gravel parking lot. Maybe a dozen units in the place in total. In the front entryway are mailboxes and a locked door that leads inside. My apartment is

Blood Gravity

on the second floor. I open the door and turn on the lights. The whole place is barely bigger than my dorm room. To the right is a small kitchen area. The rest of the place extends back in a rectangle with a small window on the far end. To the left are two doors which hide a bathroom and a closet. I unload my luggage onto the middle of the floor, and then go for a drive to find the cheapest pair of steel-toed boots available and a few groceries. Then I take a long, hot shower, and fall asleep on a pile of my clothes.

Bright and early I head to my new job. It's not much more than minimum wage, but being here feels like relief. I am no longer floating, and I am in a world my father knows nothing about. He doesn't know what I'm doing, and nothing I'm assigned to do here is anything he's ever taught me. He doesn't know these people—would not likely say two words to any of them if he saw them in passing.

I spend the morning systematically going through all the tool carts and organizing them, getting covered in grease and dirt—machine shop grease and dirt. Dirt that is not Dad's. Dirt that he'd never go near.

It's the same feeling as being in a quiet corner of a large library. Except it's not actually quiet. The machines are almost constantly running, and the employees tend to shout at each other instead of talk, but it's got that same feel like I've left the weight of everything else behind. Maybe I can be okay here.

* * *

Friday night my cell phone rings. My parents' number. I hesitate before answering, but when I do, it's Ben.

"Are you coming home this weekend?" he says.

I could say yes. It's no more than a twenty minute drive, now. But I'm not ready to see Dad just yet. I don't feel settled enough that I couldn't get knocked off-kilter.

"I'm sorry, Benny. I don't think I can make it out."

"Why not?" he whines.

"Too much to do. But I'll see you again soon, okay?"

He sniffs.

"Okay?"

"But I wanted to show you a picture I drawed." His voice is shaky, and I can almost hear the tears running down his cheeks. He sniffs again and makes an audible cry.

"Shh," I say. "I'll see it next time I come, okay? You'll keep it safe for me until then?"

"Uh-huh," he says. "When are you coming next time?"

"I don't know," I say.

"Can't you come next weekend?"

"Maybe," I say.

He cries into the receiver.

"Shh... all right, all right. I'll be there next weekend."

He stops crying and sniffs again. "Promise?"

"I promise," I say. "I'll see you in one week."

"Yay!" he says.

Dad is in the background telling Ben to say goodbye and hand off the phone.

"Bye," Ben says.

"See you soon," I say.

Then Dad gets on the line. "Hey, son."

"Hi, Dad." My heart rate speeds right on up.

"So you're coming up next weekend, then?"

"Yeah," I say.

Blood Gravity

"So how's school? How did midterms go?"

I consider lying. I consider telling the truth. I open my mouth but nothing comes out.

"Midterms?" Dad says.

I hang up the phone without uttering a word. Maybe he can think the call got dropped. A moment later the phone rings, but I let it ring and ring and go to voicemail.

Half the night I stay up, lying on my clothes-pile bed, staring at my empty apartment. But it's my empty apartment. There's a lock on the door so no one can get in. And I have no roommate. It takes a good hour before I realize what I'm feeling is safety.

I spend the weekend collecting free items from Craigslist in an effort to furnish the place. An old mattress. A small table and two chairs. A hodgepodge collection of dishes and pans. A dresser with one drawer that doesn't open. A bookshelf. I am building my own world for the first time ever.

The work week starts again on Monday. The shop begins to feel familiar. I become a new person with a new life. No one here knows where I came from. No one here knows my dad. No one here has any expectations.

At night before I go to sleep I spend my time thinking. My apartment may be small, but there is ample room for all of my thoughts and they can swim around being whatever they want to be with no one to see them.

I think about how the universe evolved over billions of years. Large clouds of hydrogen slowly contracting, forming stars. How even once a star achieves nuclear fusion, it still takes millions of years before it's stable. Everything big needs time and space to happen. Grand movements with great momentum, but nothing happening all at once. Everything builds off of what came before. Maybe here in my apartment, this is where I let time and space do their thing—here where there is no black hole.

Koa and Rachel text me a few times during the week. I tell them I'm okay. I'm just not coming back to school. Rachel wants to visit. I told her I didn't know about that just yet. I told her I need time and space right now.

Blood Gravity

CHAPTER TEN

There's a large snake on the floor between me and Ben, its head up, watching us, ready to pounce. I reach a hand towards Ben. "Come on," I say. "Move slowly. Grab my hand and step around it. I won't let it hurt you."

"I'm scared," he says. The snake probably weighs as much as he does.

Scenes from nature shows about how snakes can dislocate their jaws and swallow small farm animals whole play in the background.

"Come on, Benny. I've got you."

The room goes dark and silent. I am lying in bed. I open my eyes and look over the side and see the snake on the floor, a large lump inside of it. Jumping out of bed I grab its mouth and use everything I have to pry open its jaw, wider and wider until I can look inside and see the top of Ben's head. I dig my fingers into the snake's flesh around its jaw bones, stretching it further until the jaw tears at the corners. Soon I'm ripping the snake in half, splitting it down the middle until there's enough room to pull Ben free, but I can't tell if he's alive or not. He's not moving.

I can't breathe. I don't know what happened, why I can't get air. Maybe it's all sucked out of the room. Maybe my lungs stopped working.

Then I'm awake, back in reality, sitting bolt upright. Just a stupid dream.

Today is Friday. I promised Ben I'd come visit tonight. I can't make him cry again. But Dad will want to know about school and why I've been so difficult to reach all week. He'll grab my shoulder. He'll hug me.

I get dressed and head into work, but I keep getting distracted all day. After lunch I'm staring at a pile of metal scraps, playing out scenarios of conversations with my father in my head. Then I almost jump out of my skin when Savannah comes up behind me. "What the hell are you doing?" she says.

"Sorry."

"You've been standing here for fifteen straight minutes not moving. I thought maybe you calcified."

"No, just... a lot on my mind."

"You have work to do. Turn your mind off."

I nod and throw myself into stacking up the scraps and moving them elsewhere. She goes back into the front office.

After work I shower, put on clean clothes, and drive across town to my parents' house. As I pull into the driveway, I can already feel Dad's gravity. The familiarity of this place wants to scream at me for trying to make my own world.

Benny runs up and hugs me the second I get out of my car.

Blood Gravity

Mom hugs me as well and says, "What's with not answering your phone? I've been so worried."

"Sorry, Mom," I say. "I, uh, lost my phone."

"Well you need to talk to your father about getting a new one."

"A new what?" Dad says coming outside.

"A new phone. He lost his."

"I don't need a new phone," I say. "I'm sure it will turn up."

Dad grabs my shoulder, claiming me. But he doesn't hug this time. Maybe he senses something.

We get in the house, and Ben runs to his room, then runs back out holding a piece of paper. "This is what I drawed for you, remember?"

It's a crayon drawing of two stick people—one tall and one short. The words "Yor the best big bother" written across the top, and "luv Ben" written across the bottom.

"The best big bother, huh?" I say.

"Brother," he corrects.

I point at the word. "It's missing an r."

"Oh."

"But it's great, Benny. Thanks," I say.

Over meatloaf and potatoes, Dad says, "So you must have taken those midterms by now."

I decided earlier that I wouldn't bother lying. Like ripping off a Band-Aid, I would just get it over with. "No," I say.

"I thought they were last week."

"They were," I say.

"You didn't take them?"

"I didn't take them."

"Why not?"

I take a drink of water, set the glass down. "Because I'm not going to school anymore."

"What do you mean you're not going to school anymore?"

"I got myself a job and an apartment. I live just across the highway."

Dad drops his fork and sits up straight. His eyebrows come together. "If this is some joke, Jacob, it's not funny."

"No joke," I say.

Dad gets this look on his face like I just murdered his dreams. Dead serious, on edge, but his voice is perfectly stern and even. "You left school and you got a job and an apartment. When did you find the time to do all of this?"

"Just this last week."

"Why?"

"Because I wanted to."

Ben starts shrinking, sitting back into his seat, shoulders hunching, sliding a little lower with each passing second. Mom stares at me with this pained distress all over her face like I slapped her.

Dad says, "You're going to throw away a full-ride scholarship and a four-year degree. And for what exactly? What job is this?"

"Shop hand at a machine shop."

"Shop hand? So what, you sweep the floors?"

"Among other things," I say.

"And what does this pay? Minimum wage?"

"Ten bucks an hour," I say.

"Full time?"

I nod.

Blood Gravity

"And tell me, what's ten times forty times fifty-two?"

"Twenty-thousand, eight hundred," I say.

"So, you've run the numbers already. Tell me, what's the average starting salary for a recent college grad?"

"Something like forty-five thousand," I say.

"You think you're going to get married and raise a family on ten bucks an hour?" he says.

"I'm not getting married and raising a family."

"Why are you doing this?" Mom says. "What happened?"

Dad says, "Now you're upsetting your mother."

"You've worked so hard, and you're doing so well in school," she says, her eyes getting red.

"I'm not doing this to hurt you, Mom," I say.

Dad gets out of his seat, disappears down the hall, and returns with a Valium for Mom. He hands it to her, and down the hatch it goes.

"I get it," he nods and sits back in his seat. "I see exactly what you're doing. You're trying to rebel. Assert your independence. But this is not the way to go about it. You get a damn tattoo if you need to get it out of your system. You don't throw away your entire future."

"I'm not throwing away anything," I say. "I'm doing what I want."

Dad says, "Look, I don't know what's gotten into you, but I can tell you what you're going to do. You're quitting that job, you're leaving that apartment, and on Monday I'm driving you back to campus. We're going to talk to your professors about making up the midterm exams, and you're going to get your head out of your ass."

"Not happening," I say.

"It is happening," he says. "I'm not giving you a choice."

"It's my life. I have a choice."

"You're sitting here, telling me with a straight face, that you honestly want to drop out of school, blow your future, and work for ten goddamn bucks an hour doing a job designed for a functionally retarded person. What the hell happened?"

"You're a smart man, Dad. Maybe you can figure it out if you think hard enough."

He sits up tall. "If you have something to say to me, something to get off your chest, then find the balls and do it. Don't make some bullshit vague excuse."

Mom shakes her head in disappointment, agreeing with everything Dad says. Ben squirms in his seat like some fidgety eel.

"How many hours have I spent with you? Teaching you, encouraging you," Dad says. "You are my son. Everything I do in this life is for my children. And now you're sitting here, telling me to my face, that you're going to throw it all away like a complete moron? Is that what you are now? A goddamn moron? Is that what you've always been?"

"Maybe," I say. When he uses the word moron, I feel it in my bones. He's given me my new identity. He's deciding what I am, again. But it is stupid leaving behind a full ride scholarship and a bright future. It is stupid to throw away years of hard work.

I had pictured this playing out like some victory. I'd offend the old man, he'd get angry. I'd win for once. Instead, the look of letdown on both his and Mom's face cuts me to the core, makes me completely second guess myself. The easiest path is to say sorry, to let Dad drag me around, leaving my job and apartment, helping me get things squared away at school. I'd go back to my dorm room. I'd see Koa again. I'd see Rachel in class. My parents would still be proud of me.

It takes everything I have to say, "I'm not going back to school."

Dad finally breaks and pounds his fist hard on the table. "Christ!" He takes a breath. "Shut up!"

I close my eyes and think of my new job. I think of how Savannah got me the apartment. I have a place there. I can be okay there. I need to hold my ground.

But Ben whines as he squirms in his seat next to me. I look down as liquid drips onto the floor beneath his chair.

Mom looks him in the eye and says, "Benjamin, if you just did what I think you just did, you're in serious trouble."

Ben's eyes get red and start leaking silent, scared tears.

"Look what you made your brother do," Dad says. "You feel good about yourself now?"

Now the ache of guilt grabs hold of my lungs. I've upset Ben. He's scared. But I didn't yell. Dad yelled. But I made Dad yell.

Ben's lip quivers. I stand up, nearly knocking over my chair in the process. "Benny, you're okay," I say. "You're a big boy, right? You can go get cleaned up. Remember what we talked about?"

He nods and slowly gets out of his chair. Dad stands and attempts to follow him into the bathroom to help, but Ben says, "I can do it by myself. With privacy." Dad stops following, and Ben goes into the bathroom and locks the door, but he starts sobbing in there all by himself.

Dad turns to me. "What have you been telling him?"

Mom gets up and tries to open the bathroom door, but it's locked, so she knocks.

Ben says, "I need some privacy."

Mom says, "Open the door, Pumpkin. Let Mommy help you."

The door lock clicks and the door creaks open.

Dad looks me in the eye, his jaw tight, his eyes big and fierce. "Go. You've done enough damage for one night. We'll talk later."

In the bathroom Benny just sobs and mutters about privacy and being a big boy while Mom tries to console him. I want to check on him, but Dad stands in my way, not budging. And I know anything I might try to do or say, Dad will spin it around, cause a scene, and the kid will only get hurt more.

So I do what he wants and leave.

* * *

My apartment is quiet and cold, and I leave the lights off. All dark, like I'm out in space. I think about how long it took the solar system to form. How long it took before the asteroids were mostly confined to a belt and not knocking around into all the planets.

I touch the scabs on my stomach. Wounds heal slowly, never all at once. People grow slowly, never all at once. Large things carry momentum and it takes time and constant application of force to stop them.

What I know is I still can't say to Dad's face that he hurt me. I can't tell him what he did was wrong. I always freeze. The words stop. Because I don't know what they should be. Because I'm still not sure what it was all about.

But I left college. Possibly the dumbest decision any normal person could make, but I got away. I have my own place.

I'm making my own world.

Maybe Dad isn't a black hole. Maybe he's dark matter. He may have a gravitational pull, but he can't see me. He can't touch me.

I take Ben's drawing out of my pocket and unfold it. The two stick people. Me and Ben, who thinks I'm the "best big bother," and I put the drawing on the fridge with the lone magnet that was left by the previous tenant.

Leaving the letter r out and writing "bother" may have been a slip on Ben's part, but maybe there's something to be said for it. "Bother" doesn't just mean to annoy, it also means to make the effort to do something. If only I knew what that something was.

When I can't sleep, I leave the apartment and go for a drive, parking around the corner from my parents' house. I walk the block to their place. The house is mostly dark. They're all sleeping. I sneak around back to Ben's window, glowing with the light of a tyrannosaurus lamp. I peek in at him sound asleep all tucked in his bed, thumb in his mouth.

In his five-year-old world everything is perfect. Mom and Dad love him, spoil him. He feels safe.

Only I know he's not.

I pop the screen out of his window and open it up. "Pssst. Benny, it's Jake."

He moves in his sleep, but his eyes don't open. It occurs to me calling to him from the dark outside might terrify him and make him scream. So I slip through the window and sneak into his room. I sit on the side of his bed and shake his shoulder until his eyes blink open. He smiles, sits up, and hugs me without a word.

"I want to show you something," I say. "Come on outside with me."

He gets up and follows me to the window.

"Out the window?" he says.

"Shh," I say. "We don't want to wake Mom and Dad."

I climb out first and then help him through. I carry him in my arms into the middle of the back yard, then sit down, with him in my lap. The cold night air and his fear of the dark have him clinging to me. I point up at the sky. There's a fair amount of light pollution, but we can still see the stars.

I point out the big dipper almost directly overhead. "Those stars are so far away that their light takes thousands of years to get here."

"Whoa," he says, studying the sky.

Then I say, "I'm sorry if you got scared earlier at dinner."

"I wasn't scared," he whispers.

"I didn't mean to make you have an accident."

"I tried to have privacy," he says.

"I know," I say. "Sometimes things don't always work out. You don't have to be perfect. Have you been changing in your room now with the door closed?"

"Yeah," he whispers.

"See? You're doing good."

He smiles, and his thumb goes in his mouth.

I point at the sky again. "You see that bright star there by the moon?"

He nods.

"That's not a star at all. It's a planet. That's Jupiter. You know it's even bigger than Earth?"

"Are there dinosaurs there?" he says.

"Maybe."

"Can we go there?"

"We'd have to build a rocket ship first."

All we need is time and space and we can make our own solar system. Ben can be the sun. I orbit him, tidally locked, always watching. The dark matter all around, maybe. But it can't touch us.

Did you enjoy this story?

Rate it and/or review it online, and tell your friends! The success of these characters depends on you.

Why is this important? Because there is more to the story.

Blood Gravity is a prequel to the novel series *Scars*, which explores the relationship of these brothers as Ben comes of age and they process the betrayal of their father and their own ideas of sex, relationships, and family. For more information about this series and to subscribe to updates, visit gayletowell.com/scars where you can also find links to excerpts, associated short stories, artwork, and more!

CPSIA information can be obtained at www.ICGtesting.com
Printed in the USA
BVOW01s0224080914

365562BV00001BA/4/P